"It's wr

when we broke down

"Sorry?" Ballard says.

"It's saying we're just these soft computers. With faces."
Ballard shuts off the terminal.

"That's right," she says. "And some of us may even be losing those."

— from *A Niche*

Is this what Stuart MacLennan's doctorswere duelling with when they pumped him full of poison? It doesn't look like any tumour the coroner's seen.

For one thing and this is really kind of strange it's looking *back* at him.

— from *The Second Coming of Jasmine Fitzgerald*

"Uh, live?" Emotions squabble in Doug's cortex. The pain of failure. The hope of salvation. And now, a vague discomfort. "I don't know. I mean, they *are* okay with this, aren't they? The whole whale show thing?"

"Mr. Largha, not only are they okay with it it was their idea. So how about it? A conversation with a real, alien intelligence?"

— from *Bulk Food*

Slowly, smooth as an oiled machine, she lowers her eyes to earth and switches off the receiver. It hardly matters any more. The thunder is continuous, the wind is an incessant roar, the first hailstones are pelting down on us. If we stay out here we'll be dead in two hours. Doesn't she know it? Is this some sort of test, am I supposed to prove my love for her by facing down God like this?

— from *Nimbus*

Ten Monkeys, Ten Minutes

Peter Watts

TESSERACT BOOKS
an imprint of
THE BOOKS COLLECTIVE
EDMONTON

Copyright © 2000 Peter Watts

See page 168 for publication history of the stories in this volume.

Tesseract Books and The Books Collective acknowledge the ongoing support of the Canada Council for the Arts and the Edmonton Arts Council. Thanks to Ingénieuse Productions and to Advance Graphic Art Services Ltd. Thanks to Kim Lundquist at Priority Printing.

Editors for the press: Candas Jane Dorsey and Timothy J. Anderson
Cover art and design by Gerry Dotto.
Page design and typography by Jason Bartlett.
Printed by Priority Printing Ltd. in Edmonton.

The text of this book was set in *Adobe Janson Text* (11/12.5). This version of Janson comes from the Stempel foundry and was designed from the original type; it was issued by Linotype in digital form in 1985. The Titles are set in *Emgire Dead History Bold*. Started by P. Scott Makela while studying in the graduate design program at Cranbrook, the font was originally based on Linotypes's Centennial and Adobe's V.A.G. Rounded.

Published in Canada by Tesseract Books, an imprint of
    The Books Collective
    214-21, 10405 Jasper Avenue
    Edmonton, Alberta T5J 3S2.
    Telephone (780) 448-0590 Fax (780) 448-0640

Canadian Cataloguing in Publication Data

Watts, Peter, 1958-
    Ten monkeys, ten minutes

     ISBN 1-895836-76-X (bound) -- ISBN 1-895836-74-3 (pbk.)

  I. Title.
PS8595.A8758T46 2000 C813'.6 C00-911273-1
PR9199.3.W386T46

Ten Monkeys, Ten Minutes

THE NEW TYPE OF BOOK STORE

Fair's Fair is Calgary's new type of bookstore with five bright, clean stores housing more than 500,000 pre-owned books in very good condition. Each store's inventory is organized and searchable by computer so we can find your book quickly.

Our focus is literacy, recycling quality books and supporting the community. Fair's Fair is a Calgary owned and operated company which has been serving Calgarians for more than 20 years.

We do assist local charities and social organizations with fund raising by hosting special "open-late" evenings at our stores in which a proportion of the sales are donated to their worthwhile causes.

If you would like further information on this or other partnerships Fair's Fair offers please call:

Fair's Fair (For Book Lovers) Inc.

INGLEWOOD
907 9th Avenue SE, Calgary, AB T2G 0S5
(403) 237-8156
Corner of 9th Avenue & 8th Street SE
Mon-Sat 10 am - 6 pm, Sun 10 am - 5 pm

MOUNT ROYAL
1609 14th Street SW, Calgary, AB T3C 1E4
(403) 245-2778
Corner of 14th Street & 17th Avenue SW
Tues-Sat 10 am - 9 pm, Sun & Mon 10 am - 6 pm

MACLEOD TRAIL
7400 Macleod Trail S, Calgary, AB T2H 0L9
(403) 269-7778
Corner of 73rd Avenue & Macleod Trail S
Mon-Sat 10 am - 6 pm, Sun 10 am - 5 pm

RANCHLANDS
1829 Ranchlands Blvd NW, Calgary, AB T3G 2A7
(403) 241-2926
Across Nosehill Drive from Crowfoot Mall
Mon-Sat 10 am - 6 pm, Sun 10 am - 5 pm

CHINOOK C-TRAIN
104 61 Ave SW, Calgary, T2H 0B2
(403) 255-4011
200 metres east of Chinook station
Tues-Sat 10 am - 6 pm

Website: www.fairsfair.com
Email: gfairsfair@yahoo.com

A Niche

When the lights go out in Beebe Station, you can hear the metal groan.

Lenie Clarke lies on her bunk, listening. Overhead, past pipes and wires and eggshell plating, three kilometers of black ocean try to crush her. She feels the Rift underneath, tearing open the seabed with strength enough to move a continent. She lies there in that fragile refuge and she hears Beebe's armor shifting by microns, hears its seams creak not quite below the threshold of human hearing. God is a sadist on the Juan de Fuca Rift, and His name is Physics.

How did they talk me into this? she wonders. *Why did I come down here?* But she already knows the answer.

She hears Ballard moving out in the corridor. Clarke envies Ballard. Ballard never screws up, always seems to have her life under control. She almost seems *happy* down here.

Clarke rolls off her bunk and fumbles for a switch. Her cubby floods with dismal light. Pipes and access panels crowd the wall beside her; aesthetics run a distant second to functionality when you're three thousand meters down. She turns and catches sight of a slick black amphibian in the bulkhead mirror.

It still happens, occasionally. She can sometimes forget what they've done to her.

It takes a conscious effort to feel the machines lurking where her left lung used to be. She's so acclimated to the chronic ache in her chest, to that subtle inertia of plastic and metal as she moves, that she's scarcely aware of them any more. She can still feel the memory of what it was to be fully human, and mistake that ghost for honest sensation.

Such respites never last. There are mirrors everywhere in Beebe; they're supposed to increase the apparent size of one's personal space. Sometimes Clarke shuts her eyes to hide from the reflections forever being thrown back at her. It doesn't help. She clenches her lids and feels the corneal caps beneath them, covering her eyes like smooth white cataracts.

She climbs out of her cubby and moves along the corridor to the lounge. Ballard is waiting there, dressed in a diveskin and the usual air of confidence.

Ballard stands up. "Ready to go?"

"You're in charge," Clarke says.

"Only on paper." Ballard smiles. "No pecking order down here, Lenie. As far as I'm concerned, we're equals." After two days on the rift Clarke is still surprised by the frequency with which Ballard smiles. Ballard smiles at the slightest provocation. It doesn't always seem real.

Something hits Beebe from the outside.

Ballard's smile falters. They hear it again; a wet, muffled thud through the station's titanium skin.

"It takes a while to get used to," Ballard says, "doesn't it?"

And again.

"I mean, that sounds *big*—"

"Maybe we should turn the lights off," Clarke suggests. She knows they won't. Beebe's exterior floodlights burn around the clock, an electric campfire pushing back the darkness. They can't see it from inside — Beebe has no windows — but somehow they draw comfort from the knowledge of that unseen fire—

Thud!

—most of the time.

"Remember back in training?" Ballard says over the sound, "When they told us that the fish were usually so — small ..."

Her voice trails off. Beebe creaks slightly. They listen for a while. There's no other sound.

"It must've gotten tired," Ballard says. "You'd think they'd figure it out." She moves to the ladder and climbs downstairs.

Clarke follows her, a bit impatiently. There are sounds in Beebe that worry her far more than the futile attack of some misguided fish. Clarke can hear tired alloys negotiating surrender. She can feel the ocean looking for a way in. What if it finds one? The whole weight of the Pacific could drop down and turn her into jelly. Any time.

Better to face it outside, where she knows what's coming. All she can do in here is wait for it to happen.

Going outside is like drowning, once a day.

Clarke stands facing Ballard, diveskin sealed, in an airlock that barely holds both of them. She has learned to tolerate the forced proximity; the glassy armor on her eyes helps a bit. *Fuse seals, check headlamp, test injector*; the ritual takes her, step by reflexive step, to that horrible moment when she awakens the machines sleeping within her, and *changes*.

When she catches her breath, and loses it.

When a vacuum opens, somewhere in her chest, that swallows the air she holds. When her remaining lung shrivels in its cage, and her guts collapse; when myoelectric demons flood her sinuses and middle ears with isotonic saline. When every pocket of internal gas disappears in the time it takes to draw a breath.

It always feels the same. The sudden, overwhelming nausea; the narrow confines of the airlock holding her erect when she tries to fall; seawater churning on all sides. Her face goes under; vision blurs, then clears as her corneal caps adjust.

She collapses against the walls and wishes she could scream. The floor of the airlock drops away like a gallows. Lenie Clarke falls writhing into the abyss.

They come out of the freezing darkness, headlights blazing, into an oasis of sodium luminosity. Machines grow everywhere at the Throat, like metal weeds. Cables and conduits spiderweb across the seabed in a dozen directions. The main pumps stand over twenty meters high, a regiment of submarine monoliths fading from sight on either side. Overhead floodlights bathe the jumbled structures in perpetual twilight.

They stop for a moment, hands resting on the line that guided them here.

"I'll never get used to it," Ballard grates in a caricature of her usual voice.

Clarke glances at her wrist thermistor. "Thirty-four Centigrade." The words buzz, metallic, from her larynx. It feels so *wrong* to talk without breathing.

Ballard lets go of the rope and launches herself into the light. After a moment, breathless, Clarke follows.

There's so much power here, so much wasted strength. Here the continents themselves do ponderous battle. Magma freezes; seawater boils; the very floor of the ocean is born by painful centimeters each year. Human machinery does not *make* energy, here at Dragon's Throat; it merely hangs on and steals some insignificant fraction of it back to the mainland.

Clarke flies through canyons of metal and rock, and knows what it is to be a parasite. She looks down. Shellfish the size of boulders, crimson worms three meters long crowd the seabed between the machines. Legions of bacteria, hungry for sulfur, lace the water with milky veils.

The water fills with a sudden terrible cry.

It doesn't sound like a scream. It sounds as though a great harp string is vibrating in slow motion. But Ballard is screaming, through some reluctant interface of flesh and metal:

"LENIE—"

Clarke turns in time to see her own arm disappear into a mouth that seems impossibly huge.

Teeth like scimitars clamp down on her shoulder. Clarke stares into a scaly black face half a meter across. Some tiny dispassionate part of her searches for eyes in that monstrous fusion of spines and teeth and gnarled flesh, and fails. *How can it see me?* she wonders.

Then the pain reaches her.

She feels her arm being wrenched from its socket. The creature thrashes, shaking its head back and forth, trying to tear her into chunks. Every tug sets her nerves screaming.

She goes limp. *Please get it over with if you're going to kill me just please God make it quick* — She feels the urge to vomit, but the 'skin over her mouth and her own collapsed insides won't let her.

She shuts out the pain. She's had plenty of practice. She pulls inside, abandoning her body to ravenous vivisection; and from far away she feels the twisting of her attacker grow suddenly erratic. There's another creature at her side, with arms and legs and a knife — *you know, a knife, like the one you've got strapped to your leg and completely forgot about* — and suddenly the monster is gone, its grip broken.

Clarke tells her neck muscles to work. It's like operating a marionette. Her head turns. She sees Ballard locked in combat with something as big as she is. Only — Ballard is tearing it to pieces, with her bare hands. Its icicle teeth splinter and snap. Dark icewater courses from its wounds, tracing mortal convulsions with smoke-trails of suspended gore.

The creature spasms weakly. Ballard pushes it away. A dozen smaller fish dart into the light and begin tearing at the carcass. Photophores along their sides flash like frantic rainbows.

Clarke watches from the other side of the world. The pain in her side keeps its distance, a steady, pulsing ache. She looks; her arm is still there. She can even move her fingers without any trouble. *I've had worse*, she thinks.

Then: *Why am I still alive?*

Ballard appears at her side; her lens-covered eyes shine like photophores themselves.

"Jesus Christ," Ballard says in a distorted whisper. "Lenie? You okay?"

Clarke dwells on the inanity of the question for a moment. But surprisingly, she feels intact. "Yeah."

And if not, she knows, it's her own damn fault. She just lay there. She just waited to die. She was asking for it.

She's always asking for it.

Back in the airlock, the water recedes around them. And within them; Clarke's stolen breath, released at last, races back along visceral channels, reinflating lung and gut and spirit.

Ballard splits the face seal on her 'skin and her words tumble into the wetroom. "Jesus. Jesus! I don't believe it! My God, did you see that thing! They get so huge around here!" She passes her hands across her face; her corneal caps come off, milky hemispheres dropping from enormous hazel eyes. "And to think they're usually just a few centimeters long ..."

She starts to strip down, unzipping her 'skin along the forearms, talking the whole time. "And yet it was almost fragile, you know? Hit it hard enough and it just came apart! Jesus!" Ballard always removes her uniform indoors. Clarke suspects she'd rip the recycler out of her own thorax if she could, throw it in a corner with the 'skin and the eyecaps until the next time it was needed.

Maybe she's got her other lung in her cabin, Clarke muses. *Maybe she keeps it in a jar, and she stuffs it back into her chest at night* … She feels a bit dopey; probably just an aftereffect of the neuroinhibitors her implants put out whenever she's outside. *Small price to pay to keep my brain from shorting out — I really shouldn't mind* …

Ballard peels her 'skin down to the waist. Just under her left breast, the electrolyser intake pokes out through her ribcage.

Clarke stares vaguely at that perforated disk in Ballard's flesh. *The ocean goes into us there*, she thinks. The old knowledge seems newly significant, somehow. *We suck it into us and steal its oxygen and spit it out again.*

Prickly numbness is spreading, leaking through her shoulder into her chest and neck. Clarke shakes her head, once, to clear it.

She sags suddenly, against the hatchway.

Am I in shock? Am I fainting?

"I mean —" Ballard stops, looks at Clarke with an expression of sudden concern. "Jesus, Lenie. You look terrible. You shouldn't have told me you were okay if you weren't."

The tingling reaches the base of Clarke's skull. "I'm — okay," she says. "Nothing broke. I'm just bruised."

"Garbage. Take off your 'skin."

Clarke straightens, with effort. The numbness recedes a bit. "It's nothing I can't take care of myself."

Don't touch me. Please don't touch me.

Ballard steps forward without a word and unseals the 'skin around Clarke's forearm. She peels back the material and exposes an ugly purple bruise. She looks at Clarke with one raised eyebrow.

"Just a bruise," Clarke says. "I'll take care of it, really. Thanks anyway." She pulls her hand away from Ballard's ministrations.

Ballard looks at her for a moment. She smiles ever so slightly.

"Lenie," she says, "there's no need to feel embarrassed."

"About what?"

"You know. Me having to rescue you. You going to pieces when that thing attacked. It was perfectly understandable. Most people have a rough time adjusting. I'm just one of the lucky ones."

Right. You've always been one of the lucky ones, haven't you? I know your kind, Ballard, you've never failed at anything …

"You don't have to feel ashamed about it," Ballard reassures her.

"I don't," Clarke says, honestly. She doesn't feel much of anything any more. Just the tingling. And the tension. And a vague sort of wonder that she's even alive.

The bulkhead is sweating.

The deep sea lays icy hands on the metal and, inside, Clarke watches the humid atmosphere bead and run down the wall. She sits rigid on her bunk under dim fluorescent light, every wall of the cubby within easy reach. The ceiling is too low. The room is too narrow. She feels the ocean compressing the station around her.

And all I can do is wait …

The anabolic salve on her injuries is warm and soothing. Clarke probes the purple flesh of her arm with practiced fingers. The diagnostic tools in the Med cubby have vindicated her. She's lucky, this time; bones intact, epidermis unbroken. She seals up her 'skin, hiding the damage.

She shifts on the pallet, turns to face the inside wall. Her reflection stares back at her through eyes like frosted glass. She watches the image, admires its perfect mimicry of each movement. Flesh and phantom move together, bodies masked, faces neutral.

That's me, she thinks. *That's what I look like now.* She tries to read what lies behind that glacial facade. *Am I bored, horny, upset?* How to tell, with her eyes hidden behind those corneal opacities? She sees no trace of the tension she always feels. *I could be terrified. I could be pissing in my 'skin and no one would know.*

She leans forward. The reflection comes to meet her. They stare at each other, white to white, ice to ice. For a moment, they almost forget Beebe's ongoing war against pressure. For a moment, they don't mind the claustrophobic solitude that grips them.

How many times, Clarke wonders, *have I wanted eyes as dead as these?*

Beebe's metal viscera crowd the corridor beyond her cubby. Clarke can barely stand erect. A few steps bring her into the lounge.

Ballard, back in shirtsleeves, is at one of the library terminals. "Rickets," she says.

"What?"

"Fish down here don't get enough trace elements. They're rotten with deficiency diseases. Doesn't matter how fierce they are. They bite too hard, they break their teeth on us."

Clarke stabs buttons on the food processor; the machine grumbles at her touch. "I thought there was all sorts of food at the rift. That's why things got so big."

"There's a lot of food. Just not very good quality."

A vaguely edible lozenge of sludge oozes from the processor onto Clarke's plate. She eyes it for a moment. *I can relate.*

"You're going to eat in your gear?" Ballard asks, as Clarke sits down at the lounge table.

Clarke blinks at her. "Yeah. Why?"

"Oh, nothing. It would just be nice to talk to someone with pupils in their eyes, you know?"

"Sorry. I can take them off if you—"

"No, it's no big thing. I can live with it." Ballard turns off the library and sits down across from Clarke. "So, how do you like the place so far?"

Clarke shrugs and keeps eating.

"I'm glad we're only down here for a year," Ballard says. "This place could get to you after a while."

"It could be worse."

"Oh, I'm not complaining. I was looking for a challenge, after all. What about you?"

"Me?"

"What brings you down here? What are you looking for?"

Clarke doesn't answer for a moment. "I don't know, really,"

she says at last. "Privacy, I guess."

Ballard looks up. Clarke stares back, her face neutral.

"Well, I'll leave you to it, then," Ballard says pleasantly.

Clarke watches her disappear down the corridor. She hears the sound of a cubby hatch hissing shut.

Give it up, Ballard, she thinks. *I'm not the sort of person you really want to know.*

Almost start of the morning shift. The food processor disgorges Clarke's breakfast with its usual reluctance. Ballard, in Communications, is just getting off the phone. A moment later she appears in the hatchway.

"Management says—" She stops. "You've got blue eyes."

Clarke smiles faintly. "You've seen them before."

"I know. It's just kind of surprising, it's been a while since I've seen you without your caps in."

Clarke sits down with her breakfast. "So, what does Management say?"

"We're on schedule. Rest of the crew comes down in three weeks, we go online in four." Ballard sits down across from Clarke. "I wonder sometimes why we're not online right now."

"I guess they just want to be sure everything works."

"Still, it seems like a long time for a dry run. And you'd think that — well, they'd want to get the geothermal program up and running as fast as possible, after all that's happened."

After Lepreau and Winshire melted down, you mean.

"And there's something else," Ballard says. "I can't get through to Piccard."

Clarke looks up. Piccard Station is anchored on the Galapagos Rift; it is not a particularly stable mooring.

"You ever meet the couple there?" Ballard asks. "Ken Lubin, Lana Cheung?"

Clarke shakes her head. "They went through before me. I never met any of the other Rifters except you."

"Nice people. I thought I'd call them up, see how things were going at Piccard, but nobody can get through."

"Line down?"

"They say it's probably something like that. Nothing serious. They're sending a 'scaphe down to check it out."

Maybe the seabed opened up and swallowed them whole, Clarke thinks. *Maybe the hull had a weak plate — one's all it would take—*

Something creaks, deep in Beebe's superstructure. Clarke looks around. The walls seem to have moved closer while she wasn't looking.

"Sometimes," she says, "I wish we didn't keep Beebe at surface pressure. Sometimes I wish we were pumped up to ambient. To take the strain off the hull." She knows it's an impossible dream; most gases kill outright when breathed at three hundred atmospheres. Even oxygen would do you in if it got above one or two percent.

Ballard shivers dramatically. "If *you* want to risk breathing ninety-nine percent hydrogen, you're welcome to it. I'm happy the way things are." She smiles. "Besides, you have any idea how long it would take to decompress afterwards?"

In the Systems cubby, something bleats for attention.

"Seismic. Wonderful." Ballard disappears into Comm. Clarke follows.

An amber line is writhing across one of the displays. It looks like the EEG of someone caught in a nightmare.

"Get your eyes back in," Ballard says. "The Throat's acting up."

They can hear it all the way to Beebe; a malign, almost electrical hiss from the direction of the Throat. Clarke follows Ballard towards it, one hand running lightly along the guide rope. The distant smudge of light that marks their destination seems wrong, somehow. The color is different. It *ripples*.

They swim into its glowing nimbus and see why. The Throat is on fire.

Sapphire auroras slide flickering across the generators. At the far end of the array, almost invisible with distance, a pillar of smoke swirls up into the darkness like a great tornado.

The sound it makes fills the abyss. Clarke closes her eyes for a moment, and hears rattlesnakes.

"Jesus!" Ballard shouts over the noise. "It's not supposed to *do* that!"

Clarke checks her thermistor. It won't settle; water temperature goes from four degrees to thirty eight and back again, within seconds. A myriad ephemeral currents tug at them as they watch.

"Why the light show?" Clarke calls back.

"I don't know!" Ballard answers. "Bioluminescence, I guess! Heat-sensitive bacteria!"

Without warning, the tumult dies.

The ocean empties of sound. Phosphorescent spiderwebs wriggle dimly on the metal and vanish. In the distance, the tornado sighs and fragments into a few transient dust devils.

A gentle rain of black soot begins to fall in the copper light.

"Smoker," Ballard says into the sudden stillness. "A *big* one."

They swim to the place where the geyser erupted. There's a fresh wound in the seabed, a gash several meters long, between two of the generators.

"This wasn't supposed to happen," Ballard says. "That's why they built here, for crying out loud! It was supposed to be stable!"

"The rift's never stable," Clarke replies. *Not much point in being here if it was.*

Ballard swims up through the fallout and pops an access plate on one of the generators. "Well, according to this there's no damage," she calls down, after looking inside. "Hang on, let me switch channels here—"

Clarke touches one of the cylindrical sensors strapped to her waist, and stares into the fissure. *I should be able to fit through there*, she decides.

And does.

"We were lucky," Ballard is saying above her. "The other generators are okay too. Oh, wait a second; number two has a clogged cooling duct, but it's not serious. Backups can handle it until — *get out of there!*"

Clarke looks up, one hand on the sensor she's planting. Ballard stares down at her through a chimney of fresh rock.

"Are you *crazy*?" Ballard shouts. "That's an active smoker!"

Clarke looks down again, deeper into the shaft. It twists out of sight in the mineral haze. "We need temperature readings," she says, "from inside the mouth."

"Get out of there! It could go off again and fry you!"

I suppose it could at that, Clarke thinks. "It already blew," she calls back. "It'll take a while to build up a fresh head." She twists a knob on the sensor; tiny explosive bolts blast into the rock, anchoring the device.

"Get out of there, *now*!"

"Just a second." Clarke turns the sensor on and kicks up out of the seabed. Ballard grabs her arm as she emerges, starts to drag her away from the smoker.

Clarke stiffens and pulls free. "*Don't*—" *touch me!* She catches herself. "I'm out, okay? You don't have to—"

"Further." Ballard keeps swimming. "Over here."

They're near the edge of the light now, the floodlit Throat on one side, blackness on the other. Ballard faces Clarke. "Are you out of your *mind*? We could have gone back to Beebe for a drone! We could have planted it on remote!"

Clarke doesn't answer. She sees something moving in the distance behind Ballard. "Watch your back," she says.

Ballard turns, and sees the gulper sliding toward them. It undulates through the water like brown smoke, silent and endless; Clarke can't see the creature's tail, although several meters of serpentine flesh have come out of the darkness.

Ballard goes for her knife. After a moment, Clarke does too.

The gulper's jaw drops open like a great jagged scoop.

Ballard begins to launch herself at the thing, knife upraised.

Clarke puts her hand out. "Wait a minute. It's not coming at us."

The front end of the gulper is about ten meters distant now. Its tail pulls free of the murk.

"Are you crazy?" Ballard moves clear of Clarke's hand, still watching the monster.

"Maybe it isn't hungry," Clarke says. She can see its eyes, two tiny unwinking spots glaring at them from the tip of the snout.

"They're *always* hungry. Did you sleep through the briefings?"

The gulper closes its mouth and passes. It extends around them now, in a great meandering arc. The head turns back to look at them. It opens its mouth.

"Fuck this," Ballard says, and charges.

Her first stroke opens a meter-long gash in the creature's side.

The gulper stares at Ballard for a moment, as if astonished. Then, ponderously, it thrashes.

Clarke watches without moving. *Why can't she just let it go? Why does she always have to prove she's better than everything?*

Ballard strikes again; this time she slashes into a great tumorous swelling that has to be the stomach.

She frees the things inside.

They spill out through the wound; two huge giganturids and some misshapen creature Clarke doesn't recognize. One of the giganturids is still alive, and in a foul mood. It locks its teeth around the first thing it encounters.

Ballard. From behind.

"*Lenie!*" Ballard's knife hand is swinging in staccato arcs. The giganturid begins to come apart. Its jaws remain locked. The convulsing gulper crashes into Ballard and sends her spinning to the bottom.

Finally, Clarke begins to move.

The gulper collides with Ballard again. Clarke moves in low, hugging the bottom, and pulls the other woman clear.

Ballard's knife continues to dip and twist. The giganturid is a mutilated wreck behind the gills, but its grip remains unbroken. Ballard can't twist around far enough to reach the skull. Clarke comes in from behind and takes the creature's head in her hands.

It stares at her, malevolent and unthinking.

"Kill it!" Ballard shouts. "Jesus, what are you waiting for?"

Clarke closes her eyes, and clenches. The skull in her hand splinters like cheap plastic.

There is a silence.

After a while, she looks up. The gulper is gone, fled back into darkness to heal or die. But Ballard's still there, and Ballard is angry.

"What's *wrong* with you?" she says.

Clarke unclenches her fists. Bits of bone and jellied flesh float about her fingers.

"You're supposed to back me up! Why are you so damned — *passive* all the time?"

"Sorry." *Sometimes it works.*

Ballard reaches behind her back. "I'm cold. I think it punctured my diveskin—"

Clarke swims behind her and looks. "A couple of holes. How are you otherwise? Anything feel broken?"

"It broke through the diveskin," Ballard says, as if to herself. "And when that gulper hit me, it could have—" She turns to Clarke and her voice, even distorted, carries a shocked uncertainty. "—I could have been killed. I could have been *killed*!"

For an instant, it's as though Ballard's 'skin and eyes and self-assurance have all been stripped away. For the first time Clarke can see through to the weakness beneath, growing like a delicate tracery of hairline cracks.

You can screw up too, Ballard. It isn't all fun and games. You know that now.

It hurts, doesn't it?

Somewhere inside, the slightest touch of sympathy. "It's okay," Clarke says. "Jeanette, it's—"

"You *idiot!*" Ballard hisses. She stares at Clarke like some malign and sightless old woman. "You just floated there! You just let it happen to me!"

Clarke feels her guard snap up again, just in time. *This isn't just anger,* she realizes. *This isn't just the heat of the moment. She doesn't like me. She doesn't like me at all.*

And then, dully surprised that she hasn't seen it before:

She never did.

Beebe Station floats tethered above the seabed, a gunmetal-gray planet ringed by a belt of equatorial floodlights. There's an airlock for divers at the south pole and a docking hatch for 'scaphes at the north. In between there are girders and anchor lines, conduits and cables, metal armor and Lenie Clarke.

She's doing a routine visual check on the hull; standard procedure, once a week. Ballard is inside, testing some equipment in the communications cubby. This is not entirely within the spirit of the buddy system. Clarke prefers it this way. Relations have been civil over the past couple of days — Ballard even resurrects her patented chumminess on occasion — but the more time they spend together, the more forced things get. Eventually, Clarke knows, something is going to break.

Besides, out here it seems only natural to be alone.

She's examining a cable clamp when a razormouth charges into the light. It's about two meters long, and hungry. It rams directly into the nearest of Beebe's floodlamps, mouth agape. Several teeth shatter against the crystal lens. The razormouth twists to one side, knocking the hull with its tail, and swims off until barely visible against the dark.

Clarke watches, fascinated. The razormouth swims back and forth, back and forth, then charges again.

The flood weathers the impact easily, doing more damage to its attacker. Over and over again the fish batters itself against the light. Finally, exhausted, it sinks twitching down to the muddy bottom.

"Lenie? Are you okay?"

Clarke feels the words buzzing in her lower jaw. She trips the sender in her diveskin: "I'm okay."

"I heard something out there," Ballard says. "I just wanted to make sure you were—"

"I'm fine," Clarke says. "Just a fish."

"They never learn, do they?"

"No. I guess not. See you later."

"See—"

Clarke switches off her receiver.

Poor stupid fish. How many millennia did it take for them to learn that bioluminescence equals food? How long will Beebe have to sit here before they learn that electric light doesn't?

We could keep our headlights off. Maybe they'd leave us alone—

She stares out past Beebe's electric halo. There is so much blackness there. It almost hurts to look at it. Without lights, without sonar, how far could she go into that viscous shroud and still return?

Clarke kills her headlight. Night edges a bit closer, but Beebe's lights keep it at bay. Clarke turns until she's face to face with the darkness. She crouches like a spider against Beebe's hull.

She pushes off.

The darkness embraces her. She swims, not looking back, until her legs grow tired. She doesn't know how far she's come.

But it must be light-years. The ocean is full of stars.

Behind her, the station shines brightest, with coarse yellow rays. In the opposite direction, she can barely make out the Throat, an insignificant sunrise on the horizon.

Everywhere else, living constellations punctuate the dark. Here, a string of pearls blink sexual advertisements at two-second intervals. Here, a sudden flash leaves diversionary afterimages swarming across Clarke's field of view; something flees under cover of her momentary blindness. There, a counterfeit worm twists lazily in the current, invisibly tied to the roof of some predatory mouth.

There are so many of them.

She feels a sudden surge in the water, as if something big has just passed very close. A delicious thrill dances through her body. *It nearly touched me*, she thinks. *I wonder what it was.* The rift is full of monsters who don't know when to quit. It doesn't matter how much they eat. Their voracity is as much a part of them as their elastic bellies, their unhinging jaws. Ravenous dwarves attack giants twice their own size, and sometimes win. The abyss is a desert; no one can afford the luxury of waiting for better odds.

But even a desert has oases, and sometimes the deep hunters find them. They come upon the malnourishing abundance of the rift and gorge themselves; their descendants grow huge and bloated over such delicate bones—

My light was off, and it left me alone. I wonder—

She turns it back on. Her vision clouds in the sudden glare, then clears. The ocean reverts to unrelieved black. No nightmares accost her. The beam lights empty water wherever she points it.

She switches it off. There's a moment of absolute darkness while her eyecaps adjust to the reduced light. Then the stars come out again.

They are so beautiful. Lenie Clarke rests on the bottom of the ocean and watches the abyss sparkle around her. And she almost laughs as she realizes, three thousand meters from the nearest sunlight, that it's only dark when the lights are on.

"What the hell is wrong with you? You've been gone for over three hours, did you know that? Why didn't you answer me?"

Clarke bends over and removes her fins. "I guess I turned my receiver off," she says. "I was — wait a second, did you say—"

"You *guess*? Have you forgotten every safety reg they drilled into us? You're supposed to have your receiver on from the moment you leave Beebe until you get back!"

"Did you say *three hours*?"

"I couldn't even come out after you, I couldn't find you on sonar! I just had to sit here and hope you'd show up!"

It only seems a few minutes since she pushed off into the darkness. Clarke climbs up into the lounge, suddenly chilled.

"Where *were* you, Lenie?" Ballard demands, coming up behind her. Clarke hears the slightest plaintive tone in her voice.

"I — I must've been on the bottom," Clarke says. "that's why sonar didn't get me. I didn't go far."

Was I asleep? What was I doing for three hours?

"I was just — wandering around. I lost track of the time. I'm sorry."

"Not good enough. Don't do it again."

There's a brief silence. It's ended by the sudden, familiar impact of flesh on metal.

"Christ!" Ballard snaps. "I'm turning the externals off right now!"

Whatever it is gets in two more hits by the time Ballard reaches Comm. Clarke hears her punch a couple of buttons.

Ballard comes back into the lounge. "There. Now we're invisible."

Something hits them again. And again.

"Or maybe not," Clarke says.

Ballard stands in the lounge, listening to the rhythm of the assault. "They don't show up on sonar," she says, almost whispering. "Sometimes, when I hear them coming at us, I tune it down to extreme close range. But it looks right through them."

"No gas bladders. Nothing to bounce an echo off of."

"We show up just fine out there, most of the time. But not those things. You can't find them, no matter how high you turn the gain. They're like ghosts."

"They're not ghosts." Almost unconsciously, Clarke has been counting the beats: *eight — nine—*

Ballard turns to face her. "They've shut down Piccard," she says, and her voice is small and tight.

"What?"

"The grid office says it's just some technical problem. But I've got a friend in Personnel. I phoned him when you were outside. He says Lana's in the hospital. And I get the feeling—" Ballard shakes her head. "It sounded like Ken Lubin did something down there. I think maybe he attacked her."

Three thumps from outside, in rapid succession. Clarke can feel Ballard's eyes on her. The silence stretches.

"Or maybe not," Ballard says. "We got all those personality tests. If he was violent, they would've picked it up before they sent him down."

Clarke watches her, listens to the pounding of an intermittent fist.

"Or maybe — maybe the rift *changed* him somehow. Maybe they misjudged the pressure we'd all be under. So to speak." Ballard musters a feeble smile. "Not the physical danger so much as the emotional stress, you know? Everyday things. Just being outside could get to you after a while. Seawater sluicing through your chest. Not breathing for hours at a time. It's like — living without a heartbeat—"

She looks up at the ceiling; the sounds from outside are a bit more erratic, now.

"Outside's not so bad," Clarke says. *At least you're incompressible. At least you don't have to worry about the plates giving in.*

"I don't think you'd change suddenly. It would just sort of sneak up on you, little by little. And then one day you'd just wake up changed, you'd be different somehow, only you'd never have noticed the transition. Like Ken Lubin."

She looks at Clarke, and her voice drops a bit.

"And you."

"Me." Clarke turns Ballard's words over in her mind, waits for the onset of some reaction. She feels nothing but her own indifference. "I don't think you have much to worry about. I'm not the violent type."

"I know. I'm not worried about my own safety, Lenie. I'm worried about yours."

Clarke looks at her from behind the impervious safety of her lenses, and doesn't answer.

"You've changed since you came down here," Ballard says. "You're withdrawing from me, you're exposing yourself to unnecessary risks. I don't know exactly what's happening to you. It's almost like you're trying to kill yourself."

"I'm not," Clarke says. She tries to change the subject. "Is Lana Cheung all right?"

Ballard studies her for a moment. She takes the hint. "I don't know. I couldn't get any details."

Clarke feels something knotting up inside her.

"I wonder what she did to set him off?" she murmurs.

Ballard stares at her, openmouthed. "What *she* did? I can't believe you said that!"

"I only meant—"

"I know what you meant."

The outside pounding has stopped. Ballard does not relax. She stands hunched over in those strange, loose-fitting clothes that Drybacks wear, and stares at the ceiling as though she doesn't believe in the silence. She looks back at Clarke.

"Lenie, you know I don't like to pull rank, but your attitude is putting both of us at risk. I think this place is really getting to you. I hope you can get back online here, I really do. Otherwise I may have to recommend you for a transfer."

Clarke watches Ballard leave the lounge. *You're lying*, she realizes. *You're scared to death, and it's not just because I'm changing.*

It's because you are.

Clarke finds out five hours after the fact: something has changed on the ocean floor.

We sleep and the earth moves, she thinks, studying the topographic display. *And next time, or the time after, maybe it'll move right out from under us.*

I wonder if I'll have time to feel anything.

She turns at a sound behind her. Ballard is standing in the lounge, swaying slightly. Her face seems somehow disfigured by the concentric rings in her eyes, by the dark hollows around them. Naked eyes are beginning to look alien to Clarke.

"The seabed shifted," Clarke says. "There's a new outcropping about two hundred meters west of us."

"That's odd. I didn't feel anything."

"It happened about five hours ago. You were asleep."

Ballard glances up sharply. Clarke studies the haggard lines of her face. *On second thought …*

"I — would've woken up," Ballard says. She squeezes past Clarke into the cubby and checks the topographic display.

"Two meters high, twelve long," Clarke recites.

Ballard doesn't answer. She punches some commands into a keyboard; the topographic image dissolves, reforms into a column of numbers.

"Just as I thought," she says. "No heavy seismic activity for over forty-two hours."

"Sonar doesn't lie," Clarke says calmly.

"Neither does seismo," Ballard answers.

There's a brief silence. There's a standard procedure for such things, and they both know what it is.

"We have to check it out," Clarke says.

But Ballard only nods. "Give me a moment to change."

They call it a squid; a jet-propelled cylinder about a meter long, with a headlight at the front end and a towbar at the back. Clarke, floating between Beebe and the seabed, checks it over with one hand. Her other hand grips a sonar pistol. She points the pistol into blackness; ultrasonic clicks sweep the night, give her a bearing.

"That way," she says, pointing.

Ballard squeezes down on her own squid's towbar. The machine pulls her away. After a moment Clarke follows.

Bringing up the rear, a third squid carries an assortment of sensors in a nylon bag.

Ballard's traveling at nearly full throttle. The lamps on her helmet and squid stab the water like twin lighthouse beacons. Clarke, her own lights doused, catches up about halfway to their destination. They cruise along a couple of meters over the muddy substrate.

"Your lights," Ballard says.

"We don't need them. Sonar works in the dark."

"Are you breaking regs for the sheer thrill of it, now?"

"The fish down here, they key on things that glow—"

"Turn your lights on. That's an order."

Clarke doesn't answer. She watches the beams beside her, Ballard's squid shining steady and unwavering, Ballard's headlamp slicing the water in erratic arcs as she moves her head—

"I told you," Ballard says, "turn your — *Christ!*"

It was just a glimpse, caught for a moment in the sweep of Ballard's headlight. She jerks her head around and it slides back out of sight. Then it looms up in the squid's beam, huge and terrible.

The abyss is grinning at them, teeth bared.

A mouth stretches across the width of the beam, extends into darkness on either side. It is crammed with conical teeth the size of human hands, and they do not look the least bit fragile.

Ballard makes a strangled sound and dives into the mud. The benthic ooze boils up around her in a seething cloud; she disappears in a torrent of planktonic corpses.

Lenie Clarke stops and waits, unmoving. She stares transfixed at that threatening smile. Her whole body feels electrified, she's never been so explicitly aware of herself. Every nerve fires and freezes at the same time. She is terrified.

But she's also, somehow, completely in control of herself. She reflects on this paradox as Ballard's abandoned squid slows and stops itself, scant meters from that endless row of teeth. She wonders at her own analytical clarity as the third squid, with its burden of sensors, decelerates past and takes up position beside Ballard's.

There in the light, the grin does not change.

Clarke raises her sonar pistol and fires. *We're here*, she realizes, checking the readout. *That's the outcropping.*

She swims closer. The smile hangs there, enigmatic and enticing. Now she can see bits of bone at the roots of the teeth, and tatters of decomposed flesh trailing from the gums.

She turns and backtracks. The cloud on the seabed is starting to settle.

"Ballard," she says in her synthetic voice.

Nobody answers.

Clarke reaches down through the mud, feeling blind, until she touches something warm and trembling.

The seabed explodes in her face.

Ballard erupts from the substrate, trailing a muddy comet's tail. Her hand rises from that sudden cloud, clasped around something glinting in the transient light. Clarke sees the knife, twists almost too late; the blade glances off her 'skin, igniting nerves along her ribcage. Ballard lashes out again. This time Clarke catches the knife-hand as it shoots past, twists it, pushes. Ballard tumbles away.

"It's me!" Clarke shouts; the vocoder turns her voice into a tinny vibrato.

Ballard rises up again, white eyes unseeing, knife still in hand.

Clarke holds up her hands. "It's okay! There's nothing here! It's dead!"

Ballard stops. She stares at Clarke. She looks over to the squids, to the smile they illuminate. She stiffens.

"It's some kind of whale," Clarke says. "It's been dead a long time."

"A — a whale?" Ballard rasps. She begins to shake.

There's no need to feel embarrassed, Clarke almost says, but doesn't. Instead, she reaches out and touches Ballard lightly on the arm. *Is this how you do it?*, she wonders.

Ballard jerks back as if scalded.

I guess not—

"Um, Jeanette—" Clarke begins.

Ballard raises a trembling hand, cutting Clarke off. "I'm okay. I want to g — I think we should get back now, don't you?"

"Okay," Clarke says. But she doesn't really mean it.

She could stay out here all day.

Ballard is at the library again. She turns, passing a casual hand over the brightness control as Clarke comes up behind her; the display darkens before Clarke can see what it is. Clarke glances at the eyephones hanging from the terminal, puzzled. If Ballard doesn't want her to see what she's reading, she could just use those.

But then she wouldn't see me coming ...

"I think maybe it was a Ziphiid," Ballard's saying. "A beaked whale. Except it had too many teeth. Very rare. They don't dive this deep."

Clarke listens, not really interested.

"It must have died and rotted further up, and then sank." Ballard's voice is slightly raised. She looks almost furtively at something on the other side of the lounge. "I wonder what the chances are of that happening."

"What?"

"I mean, in all the ocean, something that big just happening to drop out of the sky a few hundred meters away. The odds of that must be pretty low."

"Yeah. I guess so." Clarke reaches over and brightens the display. One half of the screen glows softly with luminous text. The other holds the rotating image of a complex molecule.

"What's this?" Clarke asks.

Ballard steals another glance across the lounge. "Just an old biopsych text the library had on file. I was browsing through it. Used to be an interest of mine."

Clarke looks at her. "Uh huh." She bends over and studies the display. Some sort of technical chemistry. The only thing she really understands is the caption beneath the graphic.

She reads it aloud: "True Happiness."

"Yeah. A tricyclic with four side chains." Ballard points at the screen. "Whenever you're happy, really happy, that's what does it to you."

"When did they find *that* out?"

"I don't know. It's an old book."

Clarke stares at the revolving simulacrum. It disturbs her, somehow. It floats there over that smug stupid caption, and it says something she doesn't want to hear.

You've been solved, it says. *You're mechanical. Chemicals and electricity. Everything you are, every dream, every action, it all comes down to a change of voltage somewhere, or a — what did she say — a tricyclic with four side chains—*

"It's wrong," Clarke murmurs. *Or they'd be able to fix us, when we broke down—*

"Sorry?" Ballard says.

"It's saying we're just these — soft computers. With faces."

Ballard shuts off the terminal.

"That's right," she says. "And some of us may even be losing those."

The jibe registers, but it doesn't hurt. Clarke straightens and moves towards the ladder.

"Where you going? You going outside again?" Ballard asks.

"The shift isn't over. I thought I'd clean out the duct on number two."

"It's a bit late to start on that, Lenie. The shift will be over before we're even half done." Ballard's eyes dart away again. This time Clarke follows the glance to the full-length mirror on the far wall.

She sees nothing of particular interest there.

"I'll work late." Clarke grabs the railing, swings her foot onto the top rung.

"Lenie," Ballard says, and Clarke swears she hears a tremor in that voice. She looks back, but the other woman is moving to Comm. "Well, I'm afraid I can't go with you," she's saying. "I'm in the middle of debugging one of the telemetry routines."

"That's fine," Clarke says. She feels the tension starting to rise. Beebe is shrinking again. She starts down the ladder.

"Are you sure you're okay going out alone? Maybe you should wait until tomorrow."

"No. I'm okay."

"Well, remember to keep your receiver open. I don't want you getting lost on me again—"

Clarke is in the wetroom. She climbs into the airlock and runs through the ritual. It no longer feels like drowning. It feels like being born again.

She awakens into darkness, and the sound of weeping.

She lies there for a few minutes, confused and uncertain. The sobs come from all sides, soft but omnipresent in Beebe's resonant shell. She hears nothing else except her own heartbeat.

She's afraid. She's not sure why. She wishes the sounds would go away.

Clarke rolls off her bunk and fumbles at the hatch. It opens into a semi-darkened corridor; meager light escapes from the lounge at one end. The sounds come from the other direction, from deepening darkness. She follows them through an infestation of pipes and conduits.

Ballard's quarters. The hatch is open. An emerald readout sparkles in the darkness, bestowing no detail upon the hunched figure on the pallet.

"Ballard," Clarke says softly. She doesn't want to go in.

The shadow moves, seems to look up at her. "Why won't you show it?" it says, its voice pleading.

Clarke frowns in the darkness. "Show what?"

"You know what! How — afraid you are!"

"Afraid?"

"Of being here, of being stuck at the bottom of this horrible dark ocean—"

"I don't understand," Clarke whispers. Claustrophobia begins to stir in her, restless again.

Ballard snorts, but the derision seems forced. "Oh, you understand all right. You think this is some sort of competition, you think if you can just keep it all inside you'll win somehow — but it isn't like that at all, Lenie, it isn't helping to keep it hidden like this, we've got to be able to trust each other down here or we're lost—"

She shifts slightly on the bunk. Clarke's eyes, enhanced by the caps, can pick out some details now; rough edges embroider Ballard's silhouette, the folds and creases of normal clothing, unbuttoned to the waist. She thinks of a cadaver, half-dissected, rising on the table to mourn its own mutilation.

"I don't know what you mean," Clarke says.

"I've tried to be friendly," Ballard says. "I've tried to get along with you, but you're so *cold*, you won't even admit — I mean, you *couldn't* like it down here, nobody could, why can't you just admit—"

"But I don't, I — I *hate* it in here. It's like Beebe's going to — to clench around me. And all I can do is wait for it to happen."

Ballard nods in the darkness. "Yes, yes, I know what you mean." She seems somehow encouraged by Clarke's admission. "And no matter how much you tell yourself—" She stops. "You hate it *in here?*"

Did I say something wrong? Clarke wonders.

"Outside is hardly any better, you know," Ballard says. "Outside is even worse! There's mudslides and smokers and giant fish trying to eat you all the time, you can't possibly — but — you don't mind all that, do you?"

Somehow, her tone has turned accusing. Clarke shrugs.

"No, you don't," Ballard is speaking slowly now. Her voice drops to a whisper: "You actually *like* it out there. Don't you?"

Reluctantly, Clarke nods. "Yeah. I guess so."

"But it's so — the rift can kill you, Lenie. It can kill *us*. A hundred different ways. Doesn't that scare you?"

"I don't know. I don't think about it much. I guess it does, sort of."

"Then why are you so happy out there?" Ballard cries. "It doesn't make any sense …"

I'm not exactly 'happy', Clarke thinks. "I don't know. It's not that weird, lots of people do dangerous things. What about free-fallers? What about mountain climbers?"

But Ballard doesn't answer. Her silhouette has grown rigid on the bed. Suddenly, she reaches over and turns on the cubby light.

Lenie Clarke blinks against the sudden brightness. Then the room dims as her eyecaps darken.

"Jesus Christ!" Ballard shouts at her. "You *sleep* in that fucking costume now?"

It's something else Clarke hasn't thought about. It just seems easier.

"All this time I've been pouring my heart out to you and you've been wearing that *machine's* face! You don't even have the decency to show me your goddamned *eyes!*"

Clarke steps back, startled. Ballard rises from the bed and takes a single step forward. "To think you could actually pass for human before they gave you that suit! Why don't you go find something to play with out in your fucking ocean!"

And slams the hatch in Clarke's face.

Lenie Clarke stares at the sealed bulkhead for a few moments. Her face, she knows, is calm. Her face is usually calm. But she stands there, unmoving, until the cringing thing inside of her unfolds a little.

"Okay," she says at last, very softly. "I guess I will."

Ballard is waiting for her as she emerges from the airlock. "Lenie," she says quietly, "we have to talk. It's important."

Clarke bends over and removes her fins. "Go ahead."

"Not here. In my cubby."

Clarke looks at her.

"Please."

Clarke starts up the ladder.

"Aren't you going to take—" Ballard stops as Clarke looks down. "Never mind. It's okay."

They ascend into the lounge. Ballard takes the lead. Clarke follows her down the corridor and into her cabin. Ballard dogs the hatch and sits on her bunk, leaving room for Clarke.

Clarke looks around the cramped space. Ballard has curtained over the mirrored bulkhead with a spare sheet.

Ballard pats the bed beside her. "Come on, Lenie. Sit down."

Reluctantly, Clarke sits. Ballard's sudden kindness confuses her. Ballard hasn't acted this way since …

… *Since she had the upper hand.*

"—might not be easy for you to hear," Ballard is saying, "but we have to get you off the rift. They shouldn't have put you down here in the first place."

Clarke doesn't reply.

"Remember the tests they gave us?" Ballard continues. "They

measured our tolerance to stress; confinement, prolonged isolation, chronic physical danger, that sort of thing."

Clarke nods slightly. "So?"

"So," says Ballard, "Did you think for a moment they'd test for those qualities without knowing what sort of person would have them? Or how they got to be that way?"

Inside, Clarke goes very still. Outside, nothing changes.

Ballard leans forward a bit. "Remember what you said? About mountain climbers, and free-fallers, and why people deliberately do dangerous things? I've been reading up, Lenie. Ever since I got to know you I've been reading up—"

Got to know me?

"—and do you know what thrillseekers have in common? They all say that you haven't lived until you've nearly died. They need the danger. It gives them a rush."

You don't know me at all—

"Some of them are combat veterans, some were hostages for long periods, some just spent a lot of time in dead zones for one reason or another. And a lot of the really compulsive ones—"

Nobody knows me.

"—the ones who can't be happy unless they're on the edge, all the time — a lot of them got started early, Lenie. When they were just children. And you, I bet — you don't even like being touched—"

Go away. Go away.

Ballard puts her hand on Clarke's shoulder. "How long were you abused, Lenie?" she asks gently. "How many years?"

Clarke shrugs off the hand and does not answer. *He didn't mean any harm.* She shifts on the bunk, turning away slightly.

"That's it, isn't it? You don't just have a tolerance to trauma, Lenie. You've got an *addiction* to it. Don't you?"

It only takes Clarke a moment to recover. The 'skin, the eyecaps make it easier. She turns calmly back to Ballard. She even smiles a little.

"*Abused*," she says. "Now *there's* a quaint term. Thought it died out after the Saskatchewan witch-hunts. You some sort of history buff, Jeanette?"

"There's a mechanism," Ballard tells her. "I've been reading about it. Do you know how the brain handles stress, Lenie? It dumps all sorts of addictive stimulants into the bloodstream. Beta-endorphins, opioids. If it happens often enough, for long enough, you get hooked. You can't help it."

Clarke feels a sound in her throat, a jagged coughing noise a bit like tearing metal. After a moment, she recognizes it as laughter.

"I'm not making it up!" Ballard insists. "You can look it up yourself if you don't believe me! Don't you know how many abused children spend their whole lives hooked on wife beaters or self-mutilation or free-fall—"

"And it makes them happy, is that it?" Clarke says, still smiling. "They *enjoy* getting raped, or punched out, or—"

"No, of course you're not happy! But what *you* feel, that's probably the closest you've ever come. So you confuse the two, you look for stress anywhere you can find it. It's physiological addiction, Lenie. You ask for it. You always asked for it."

I ask for it. Ballard's been reading, and Ballard knows: Life is pure electrochemistry. No use explaining how it *feels*. No use explaining that there are far worse things than being beaten up. There are even worse things than being held down and raped by your own father. There are the times between, when nothing happens at all. When he leaves you alone, and you don't know for how long. You sit across the table from him, forcing yourself to eat while your bruised insides try to knit themselves back together; and he pats you on the head and smiles at you, and you know the reprieve's already lasted too long, he's going to come for you tonight, or tomorrow, or maybe the next day.

Of course I asked for it. How else could I get it over with?

"Listen." Clarke shakes her head. "I—" But it's hard to talk, suddenly. She knows what she wants to say; Ballard's not the only one who reads. Ballard can't see it through a lifetime of fulfilled expectations, but there's nothing special about what happened to Lenie Clarke. Baboons and lions kill their own young. Male sticklebacks beat up their mates. Even *insects* rape. It's not abuse, really, it's just — biology.

But she can't say it aloud, for some reason. She tries, and she tries, but in the end all that comes out is a challenge that sounds almost childish:

"Don't you know *anything*?"

"Sure I do, Lenie. I know you're hooked on your own pain, and so you go out there and keep daring the rift to kill you, and eventually it will, don't you see? That's why you shouldn't be here. That's why we have to get you back."

Clarke stands up. "I'm not going back." She turns to the hatch.

Ballard reaches out toward her. "Listen, you've got to stay and hear me out. There's more."

Clarke looks down at her with complete indifference. "Thanks for your concern. But I don't have to stay. I can leave any time I want to."

"You go out there now and you'll give everything away, they're watching us! Haven't you figured it out *yet*?" Ballard's voice is rising. "Listen, they *knew* about you! They were *looking* for someone like you! They've been testing us, they don't know yet what kind of person works out better down here, so they're watching and waiting to see who cracks first! This whole program is still experimental, can't you see that? Everyone they've sent down — you, me, Ken Lubin and Lana Cheung, it's all part of some cold-blooded test—"

"And you're failing it," Clarke says softly. "I see."

"They're *using* us, Lenie — *don't go out there!*"

Ballard's fingers grasp at Clarke like the suckers of an octopus. Clarke pushes them away. She undogs the hatch and pushes it open. She hears Ballard rising behind her.

"*You're sick!*" Ballard screams. Something smashes into the back of Clarke's head. She goes sprawling out into the corridor. One arm smacks painfully against a cluster of pipes as she falls.

She rolls to one side and raises her arms to protect herself. But Ballard just steps over her and stalks into the lounge.

I'm not afraid, Clarke notes, getting to her feet. *She hit me, and I'm not afraid. Isn't that odd—*

From somewhere nearby, the sound of shattering glass.

Ballard's shouting in the lounge. "The experiment's over! Come on out, you fucking ghouls!"

Clarke follows the corridor, steps out of it. Pieces of the lounge mirror hang like great jagged stalactites in their frame. Splashes of glass litter the floor.

On the wall, behind the broken mirror, a fisheye lens takes in every corner of the room.

Ballard is staring into it. "Did you hear me? I'm not playing your stupid games any more! I'm through performing!"

The quartzite lens stares back impassively.

So you were right, Clarke muses. She remembers the sheet in Ballard's cubby. *You figured it out, you found the pickups in your own cubby, and Ballard, my dear friend, you didn't tell me.*

How long have you known?

Ballard looks around, sees Clarke. "You've got *her* fooled, all right," she snarls at the fisheye, "but *she's* a goddamned basket case! She's not even sane! Your little tests don't impress *me* one fucking bit!"

Clarke steps toward her.

"Don't call me a basket case," she says, her voice absolutely level.

"That's what you *are!*" Ballard shouts. "You're sick! That's why you're down here! They *need* you sick, they depend on it, and you're so far gone you can't see it! You hide everything behind that — that *mask* of yours, and you sit there like some masochistic jellyfish and just take anything anyone dishes out — you *ask* for it—"

That used to be true, Clarke realizes as her hands ball into fists. *That's the strange thing.* Ballard begins to back away; Clarke advances, step by step. *It wasn't until I came down here that I learned that I could fight back. That I could win. The rift taught me that, and now Ballard has too—*

"Thank you," Clarke whispers, and hits Ballard hard in the face.

Ballard goes over backwards, collides with a table. Clarke calmly steps forward. She catches a glimpse of herself in a glass icicle; her capped eyes seem almost luminous.

"Oh Jesus," Ballard whimpers. "Lenie, I'm *sorry.*"

Clarke stands over her. "Don't be," she says. She sees herself as some sort of exploding schematic, each piece neatly labeled. *So much anger in here,* she thinks. *So much hate. So much to take out on someone.*

She looks at Ballard, cowering on the floor.

"I think," Clarke says, "I'll start with you."

But her therapy ends before she can even get properly

warmed up. A sudden noise fills the lounge, shrill, periodic, vaguely familiar. It takes a moment for Clarke to remember what it is. She lowers her foot.

Over in the Communications cubby, the telephone is ringing.

Jeanette Ballard is going home today.

For half an hour the 'scaphe has been dropping deeper into midnight. Now the Comm monitor shows it settling like a great bloated tadpole onto Beebe's docking assembly. Sounds of mechanical copulation reverberate and die. The overhead hatch drops open.

Ballard's replacement climbs down, already mostly 'skinned, staring impenetrably from eyes without pupils. His gloves are off; his 'skin is open up to the forearms. Clarke sees the faint scars running along his wrists, and smiles a bit inside.

Was there another Ballard up there, waiting, she wonders, in case I had been the one who didn't work out?

Out of sight down the corridor, a hatch hisses open. Ballard appears in shirtsleeves, one eye swollen shut, carrying a single suitcase. She seems about to say something, but stops when she sees the newcomer. She looks at him for a moment. She nods briefly. She climbs into the belly of the 'scaphe without a word.

Nobody calls down to them. There are no salutations, no morale-boosting small talk. Perhaps the crew have been briefed. Perhaps they've figured it out on their own. The docking hatch swings shut. With a final clank, the 'scaphe disengages.

Clarke walks across the lounge and looks into the camera. She reaches between mirror fragments and rips its power line from the wall.

We don't need this any more, she thinks, and she knows that somewhere far away, someone agrees.

She and the newcomer appraise each other with dead white eyes. "I'm Lubin," he says at last.

Ballard was right again, she realizes. *Untwisted, we'd be of no use at all …*

But she doesn't really mind. She won't be going back.

Fractals
(or: Reagan Assured Gorbachev of Help Against Space Aliens)

Trespassing? *Trespassing*? You arrogant slant-eyed alien motherfucker, I used to *live* here!

How long have I wanted to do that? How many years have I hated them, dreamt that my fists were smashing those faces into shapes even less human? I can't remember. The anger is chronic. The anger has always been chronic. And impotent, until now. The pain in my knuckles throbs like a distant badge of honour.

It's cold.

The rage is gone, absorbed somehow by the mud and the unlit piles of lumber and masonry scattered around me. I can barely focus on my surroundings. The shapes keep changing, hulking angular monstrosities shifting on all sides. Only the sign at the front of the lot, the sign he kept pointing at, refuses to move.

I can barely see him in the dark. He's just a few meters away, but the shadows are so *black* and he doesn't move at all. What if I killed him? What if I—

There. He moved a bit. It's okay, I didn't kill him, he's not dead—

Yet. What if he dies here in the mud?

(So what if he does? Lots more where he came from.)

No. I don't mean that. I can't believe I ever did, I mean, what if I, what if he dies here, what if—

What if he lives, and identifies me?

A couple of steps forward. A couple more. Okay, he was about *here* when he saw me, and then he moved over *there* and started shouting—

He couldn't have seen my face. Even when he came closer, it's so dark he'd only have seen a silhouette, and then he was right in front of me and—

I can get away. I can get away. Oh Jesus God I can't believe I did this—

Okay. This is a construction site, after all; my car will only leave one set of tracks in a muddle of hundreds. And the nearest house is over a block away, this whole end of the road is unlit. Lucky me: no witnesses.

The car starts smoothly, without a moment's hesitation. I descend toward the city.

It was as though I had planned it all, somehow. In a way I feel as though I've been rehearsing this forever. I have been purged. It's such a relief not to burn, to unclench my teeth, to feel the hard knot of tension in my stomach easing away. Somehow, I'm free. Not happy, perhaps. But I have acted, at last, from the heart, and in some strange way I'm finally at peace.

(What if he dies up there?)

I'll stop at the next phone booth. Ambulances respond to anonymous tips, don't they? In the meantime, I've got to be careful to keep my shoes on the mudmat. Just in case. Joanne might still be awake when I get home. I'll stop off at a gas station and rinse everything clean on the way.

It's a nice window; nice scenery. I've always liked forests, though I've never seen so many squirrels and deer and birds crammed into such a small area before. But hey, who am I to complain about realism, I'm twenty floors over Robson Street looking out at a *rainforest* so why worry about details? Besides, it's not a rainforest any more. It's an alpine meadow. She touches a button on the windowsill and the whole world changes.

I walk across the room; rocks and heather come into view, cross the window, fall into eclipse at the other side. I move closer and the field of view expands. Nose against glass I can see one hundred and eighty, three-dimensional degrees along all axes. Just outside, an explosion of flowers stirs in a sudden breeze.

But now she fingers a switch and the world *stops*, there's no window at all any more, just a flat grey screen and a fake window sill.

"That's incredible," I say, distantly amazed.

She can't quite keep the pride out of her voice. "It's a breakthrough all right. There are other flat monitors around, but you can see the difference."

"How do you do it? Is this some sort of 3-d videotape or something?"

Her smile widens. "Not even close. We use fractals."

"Fractals."

"You know, those psychedelic patterns you see on calendars and computer posters."

Right. Something to do with chaos theory. "But what exactly *are*—"

She laughs. "Actually, I just demonstrate the stuff. We got a guy at the university to hack the software for us, he'd be able to tell you the details. If you think your readers would be interested."

"I'm interested. If I can't get them interested too I'm not much of a journalist, am I?"

"Well then, let me give you his name," she says. "I'll tell him to expect you. He should be able to set something up within the next week or so."

She jots a name on the back of her card and hands it to me. Roy Cheung, it says. I feel a sudden brief constriction in my throat.

"One last question," I say to her. "Who's going to be able to afford something like this?"

"Bottom-line models will retail at around thirty thousand," she tells me. "A lot of businesses want to hang one in their lobbies and so forth. And we also hope to sell to upper income individuals."

"If you can find any nowadays."

"You'd be surprised, actually. Since the Hong Kong influx started there's been a real surge in the number of people who can afford this sort of product."

You poor dear. You haven't done your market research, have you? Or you'd know exactly what your wealthy clientele think of nature. It's abstract art to them. There probably isn't a blade of grass left in all of Hong Kong. Most of those people wouldn't know what a tree was if one grew through their penthouse windows and spat oxygen all over the walls.

No matter. In another few years, neither will we.

"Emergency Admissions."

"Uh, yes. I was wondering if you've had — if there was an assault victim admitted over the past day or so."

"I'm sorry sir, you'll have to be more specific. Assault victim?"

"Yes, um, has someone been admitted suffering head injuries, an oriental—"

"Why?" The voice acquires a sudden sharp edge. "Do you know something about an unreported assault?"

"Uh—" Hang up, you idiot! This isn't getting you anywhere! "Actually, it must have been reported, they were loading him into an ambulance. He looked pretty bad, I was just wondering how he was doing."

Yeah. Right. Very credible.

"I see. And where did this happen?"

"North Van. Up around, um, Cumberland I think."

"And I don't suppose you know the name of the victim?"

"Uh no, like I said I just saw them taking him away, I was just wondering—"

"That's very … kind of you, sir," she says. "But we're not allowed to disclose such information except to family—"

Jesus *Christ*, woman, I just want to find out how he's doing, I'm not interested in stealing national secrets for Chrissake! "I understand that, but—"

"And in any event, nobody answering your description has been admitted to this hospital. Cumberland, you said?"

Maybe they're tracing the call. It would make sense, maybe they've got a standing trace on emergency hospital lines, I bet a lot of people do what I'm doing, I bet—

"Sir? You said Cumberland?"

I disconnect.

Joanne stirs as I slip into the darkened bedroom. "Anything interesting on the news?"

"Not really." No reports of unknown assailants on the North Shore, anyway. That's probably just as well. Wouldn't a dead body at least warrant mention?

I feel my way to the bed and climb in. "Oh, The Musqueam Indians are planning this massive demonstration over land claims. Roadblocks and everything." I mould myself against Joanne's back.

"They must hate our guts," I say into her nape.

She turns around to face me. "Who? The Musqueam?"

"They must. I would."

She makes a wry sound. "No offense, lover, but I'd be very worried if too many other people thought the way you did."

I've learned to take such remarks as compliments, although that's almost never the way she means them. "Well, if getting home and culture stolen out from under you isn't grounds for hatred, I don't know what is." I hold back a moment, decide to risk it. "I wonder if that makes them racists."

"Ooh. Shame on you." She wags a finger that I can barely make out in the darkness. "*Victims* of racism can't possibly be *guilty* of racism. Why, you'd have to be a racist to even suggest such a thing. Excuse me while I call the Human Rights Commission." Instead, she kisses me. "Actually, I'm too tired. I'll let you off with a warning. G'night." She settles down with her back to me.

But I don't want to sleep, not yet. There are things I have to say aloud, things I can't even think about without invoking some subtle, chronic dread. I don't like keeping things from Joanne. Three days now and the silence spreads through me like gangrene.

But I can't tell her. It could ruin everything. How much am I supposed to gamble on the hope she'd grant absolution?

"I saw some graffitti today on Denman," I try aloud. "It said *White man out of Vancouver. Canada now for Asian Peoples*."

Her back moves in a gentle respiratory rhythm. She mumbles something into her pillow.

I ask: "What did you say?"

"I said, there's assholes on all sides. Go to sleep."

"Maybe it's true."

She groans, defeated: if she wants any sleep tonight she'll have to hear me out. "What's true?" she sighs.

"Maybe there isn't room for all of us. I was on the bus today, it was full of all these Chinese and I couldn't understand what any of them were saying—"

"Don't sweat it. They probably weren't talking to you."

No, I want to say, they don't have to. We don't matter to them. Our quaint values and esthetics can be bought as easily as the North Shore. Don't I have a right to be afraid of that? Can't we fear for our own way of life without being racist? Aren't we even allowed to—

—beat the fuckers to death with our bare hands—

There's something else here.

It's lying in the dark between us and it's invisible, Joanne could roll over right now and she wouldn't see it any more than I can, but somehow I know it's looking right at me and *grinning* …

Joanne sits up without a word. It's as though my own inadvertent thoughts have triggered her. She turns to look at me, she leans right through the thing between us without even pausing, her face breaks through that invisible grin and replaces it with one of her own.

"If you wasn't livin' with a black woman," she says in her best Aunt Jemima drawl, "I'd say you was sho 'nuff a racist honky sumbitch." She nips me on the nose. "As it is, I think you just need a good night's sleep." She settles back down with one arm draped over my chest.

We're alone again. In the next room, Sean coughs softly in her sleep.

My knuckles sting with faint remembrance.

I wonder if he had a family.

Whoever you were. I'm—

—sorry—

It's almost time to meet Roy Cheung. For two hours now I've been wandering downtown streets, watching morning traffic congeal in thin slushy snow. I've been counting invaders. They hurry past the rest of us, mixed but not mixing, heads down against the chill of this alien climate. Sometimes they speak to each other. Sometimes they even use our language. More often they say nothing at all.

They never look at me.

I didn't always feel this way. I'm almost sure of it. There was a time when we were all just people, and I knew exactly what racism looked like: it drove a Ford pickup with a gun rack in the rear window. It threw beer bottles out the window at stop signs, and it didn't think; it gibbered.

But now statistics and xenophobia are in bed together. Every day the planes touch down and the balance shifts a little more. Asian wealth rises around us, flashing invisibly bank-to-bank, ricocheting down from comsats high over the Pacific rim. Burying us. Who wouldn't be afraid? My whole world is listing to the east.

But nobody taught me to *hate* like this. It just happened.

Is this what it's like to discover you're a werewolf?

There's a poster commemorating the 1995 International Computer Graphics Conference hanging on one wall of Roy Cheung's office. Below it, a transistor radio emits country and western; it's partially eclipsed by a huge, luxuriant Boston fern in a hanging pot. I wonder how he does it. Every time *I* buy one of those bloody plants it's dead within a week.

His desk is barely visible under a mass of printouts and the biggest colour monitor I've ever seen. There is a spiral galaxy rotating on the screen. It seems to be made of iridescent soap bubbles, each arranged with unimaginable precision.

"That," says Cheung, "is a fractal. Beautiful, isn't it?"

He speaks without a trace of accent. He sounds just like I do.

Cheung sits down at the keyboard. "Watch closely. I'm increasing the magnification so we're only looking at one of these nodes. One star in the galaxy, if you will."

The image blurs, then refocusses. There is a spiral galaxy rotating on the screen.

"That's the same image," I say.

"Not quite. There are a number of differences, but overall it's pretty similar. Except, like I said, we're only looking at one star in the galaxy."

"But that's a whole—"

"Now let's zoom in on a single star in *this* galaxy."

There is a spiral galaxy rotating on the screen.

Something clicks. "Isn't this what you call infinite regression?"

He nods. "Actually, the term is *scale-invariance*. You can look at this thing with a microscope or a telescope, it doesn't matter; at every scale, the pattern is essentially the same."

"So at what scale do we get the nature scenes?" There isn't the slightest hint of tension in my voice. I even smile.

"All of them. This fractal comes from a very simple equation; the trick is it keeps repeating itself. Uses the output from one iteration as the input for the next. You don't have to store a complete image at all. You just store a few equations and let the computer draw the picture step-by-step. You get incredibly detailed output with hardly any memory cost."

"You're saying you can duplicate nature on a screen with a bunch of simple equations?"

"No. I'm saying nature *is* a bunch of simple equations."

"Prove it," I tell him, still smiling. For an instant I see him shrouded in darkness, arms thrown up in a vain attempt to ward off judgment, face bleeding and pulpy.

I shake my head to dislodge the image. It sticks.

"—shape of a tree," he's saying. "The trunk splits into branches. Then the branches split into smaller branches. Then those divide into twigs. And at each scale, the pattern is the same."

I imagine a tree. It doesn't seem very mathematical.

"Or your own lungs," Cheung continues. "Windpipe to bronchi to bronchioles to alveoli. Or your circulatory system. Or the growth of a crystal. Incrementally simple, the same thing happening at a dozen different scales simultaneously."

"So you're saying trees are fractal? Crystals are fractal?"

He shakes his head, grinning from ear to ear. "*Nature* is fractal. *Life* is fractal. *You're* fractal." He wears the look of a religious convert. "And the image compression stuff is nothing. There are implications for meteorology, or — wait a second, let me show you what I'm working on for the medical centre."

I wait while Cheung fiddles with his machine. Voices from his radio fill the lull. A phone-in show; some woman is complaining to the host about a three-car pile-up in her front yard. Her neighbour up the hill used a garden hose to wash the snow off his driveway this morning; the water slid downhill and froze the road into a skating rink, tilted twenty degrees.

"They come in from Hong Kong, they think the climate is just the same the world over," the caller complains.

The host doesn't say anything. How can he? How can he sympathise without being branded a racist? Maybe he will anyway. Maybe he'll call a spade a spade, maybe the editors and the censors haven't quite crushed him yet. Go for it, asshole, it's what we're all thinking, why don't you just *say* it—

"What an idiot," Roy Cheung remarks.

I blink. "What?"

"That's actually pretty minor," he tells me. "That's just some moron who never saw ice outside of a scotch on the rocks. We've got these neighbours, a whole bloody family came over from Hong Kong a couple of years back and we've had nothing but trouble. Last summer they cut down our hedge."

"What?" It's very strange, hearing Cheung betray his own kind like this.

"My wife's into horticulture, she'd spent ages growing this hedge on our property. It was gorgeous, about fifteen feet high, perfectly sculpted. Came home one day and these guys had paid someone to come over and chainsaw the whole thing. Said the hedge was a home for evil spirits."

"Didn't you sue them or something?"

Cheung shrugs. "I wanted too. Lana wouldn't let me. She didn't want any more trouble. You ask me, I'd gladly ship the whole lot of 'em back overseas."

I collect my thoughts. "But didn't you, um, come from—"

"Born here. Fifth generation," he says.

I'm only third.

And suddenly I recognise the kinship behind those strange eyes, the shared resentment. How must it feel to go through life wearing that skin, that hair, these artifacts of a heritage left behind decades ago? Roy Cheung, guilty by association, probably hates them more than I do. He's almost an ally.

"Anyway," he says, "here's what I wanted to show you."

The moment passes. There is something new on the monitor, something reddish and amorphous and somehow threatening. It's growing; a misshapen blob, sprouting random pseudopods, covers half the screen.

"What's that?" I ask.

"Carcinoma."

It doesn't surprise me.

"Cancer is fractal too," Cheung says. "This is a model of a liver tumour, but the growth patterns are the same no matter what kind you're talking about. We're finding out how it grows; you gotta know that before you can kill it."

I watch it spread.

Baboons. There are baboons running around in our TV, courtesy of National Geographic and PBS. We more civilized primates sit and watch at a discreet distance. Sean, hyperactively four, bounces around on the carpet; Joanne and I opt for the couch. We peer over a coffee table laden with Szechuan takeout, into what's left of the real world.

There's just been a treetop coup somewhere in the forests of central Africa; a new alpha male struts around. He goes through the troop, checking out the females, checking out their kids. Especially the kids. He goes to each one in turn, running his big hairy hand over their heads, sniffing their bodies with that gentle paternalism, looking for some sign of familiarity, some telltale scent that speaks of *his* ancestry in those tiny bodies — but no, none of my genes in *this* one, and WHAP the infant's head snaps back and forth like a bolo-ball and SNAP those matchstick arms bend in entirely new places and the Big Man on Campus tears the little carcass away from its screaming mother and pitches it out, out and down to the forest floor twenty meters below.

Sean is suddenly entranced. Joanne looks at me doubtfully. "I don't know if we really want to be watching this during, er, mealtime …"

But life isn't always so intolerant, the narrator hastens to tell us. That same male would die defending those bastard children against an outside threat, against a predator or a rival troop, against anything that was less related to him than they were. Loyalties are concentric. Defend your kind against others. Defend your kin against your kind. Defend your genes against your kin. In absence of the greater threat, destroy the lesser.

And suddenly, with an almost audible click, the whole world drops into focus. I look around, surprised; nobody else seems to have noticed the change. On the surface, nothing *has* changed. My family is blissfully unaware of the epiphany that has just occurred.

But I understand something now. It wasn't really my fault.

Go down far enough, and we're all running the same program. Each cell holds the complete design; the framework, the plumbing, the wiring diagrams, all jammed into a spiral thread of sugars and bases that tells us what to be. What blind stupid arrogance, to think that a few campfire songs could undo four million years of evolution. *Morally wrong*, we chant; *politically incorrect, socially unacceptable*. But our genes aren't fooled. They're so much wiser than we are. They know: we have met the enemy, and he is *not* us. Evolution, ever patient, inspires us to self-defense.

My enmity is hardwired. Am I to blame if the plan calls for something that hates?

What's this? They've changed the bait again?

It can't be an easy job, trying to bribe us into literacy. Each week they put a new display in the lobby, easily visible through the glass to passers-by, some colourful new production meant to lure the great unwashed into the library.

Wasted on me; I'm in here for something else entirely. Although, what the hell, the newspaper section doesn't close for hours. And today's offering is a tad more colourful than usual. Let's see …

A crayon drawing of crude stick figures, red and yellow, black and white, holding hands in a ring. Posters, professionally craft-ed but no less blatant, showing Chinese and Caucasians wearing hard hats and smiling at each other. The air is thick with sugary sweetness and light; I feel the first stirrings of diabetes.

I move closer to the display. A sign, prominently displayed: "Sponsored by the B.C. Human Rights Commission".

They know. They have their polls, their barometers, they can feel the backlash building and they're fighting it any way they can.

I wander the exhibit. I feel a bit like a vampire at church. But the symbols here are weak; the garlic and the holy signs have an air of desperation about them. They're losing, and they know it. This feeble propaganda can't change how we feel.

Besides, why should they care what we think? In another few years we won't matter any more.

There's a newspaper clipping tacked up on one corner of the nearest board. From an old 1986 edition of the Globe and Mail: "Reagan Assured Gorbachev of Help Against Space Aliens", the headline says.

Is this for real?

Yes indeed. Then-president Reagan, briefly inspired, actually told Gorbachev that if the Earth were ever threatened by aliens, all countries would pull together and forget their ideological differences. Apparently he thought there was a moral there somewhere.

"One of the few intelligent things Reagan ever said," someone says at my elbow. I turn. She's overdressed; wears a B.C. government pin on one lapel and a button on the other. The button shows planet Earth encircled by the words "We're all in this together".

But at least she's one of us.

"But he was right," I reply. "Threaten the whole human race and our international squabbling seems so petty."

She nods, smiling. "That's why I put it up. It's not really part of the presentation, but I thought it fit."

"Of course, we don't have space aliens to hate. But not to worry. There's always an enemy, somewhere."

Her smile falters a bit. "What do you mean?"

"If not space aliens, the Russians. If not the Russians, the local ethnics. I stayed on an island once where the lobstermen on the south end all hated the herring fishermen on the north. They all seemed the same to me, a lot of them were even related, but they had to be able to hate someone *somewhere*."

She clucks and shakes her head in cynical accord.

"Of course, both sides banded together to hate all off-islanders," I add.

"Of *course*."

"A single human being, the whole damn species, or any level in between, and the pattern's the same, isn't it? It's like hatred is—"

I see galaxies within galaxies.

"—scale-invariant," I finish slowly.

She looks at me, a bit strangely. "Uh—"

"But of course, there are also a lot of positive things happening. People *can* co-operate when they have to."

Her smile reinflates. "Exactly."

"Like the natives. Banding together to save their cultures, forgetting their differences. The Haidas even stopped taking slaves from other tribes."

She isn't smiling at all now. "The Haida," she says, "haven't taken slaves for generations."

"Oh, that's right. We put a stop to that about — I guess it was even before we banned the potlatch, wasn't it? But eventually they'll want to start up again. I mean, slavery was integral to their culture, and we simply *must* protect the integrity of everyone's culture here, mustn't we?"

"I don't think you've got all your facts straight," she says slowly.

"Oh, I'm sorry. I thought we were multicultural. I thought Canadians were supposed to—" I spy some bold print a few boards down— "*to allow different cultures to flourish side by side without imposing our own moral and ethical standards on them*."

"Within the law," she says. I wait, but she's wary now, unwilling to speak further.

So I do. "Then as a woman, I'm sure you're pleased that Muslim men won't have to stop the traditional subjugation of their wives when they come here. As long as they keep it in the home, of course."

"Excuse me." She turns her back to me, takes a step along the display.

"You're lying to us," I say, raising my voice. A couple of bystanders turn their heads.

She faces me, mouth open to speak. I pre-empt her: "Or perhaps you're lying to *them*. But you can't have it both ways, and you can't change the facts no matter how many bad classroom cartoons you force on us."

There's a part of me that hasn't enjoyed provoking the anger in her face. A few days ago, it might even have been the biggest part. But it's only a few thousand years old, tops, and the rest of me really doesn't give a shit.

I lift my arm in a gesture that takes in the whole display. "If *I* were a racist," I tell her, "this wouldn't *begin* to convince me."

I bare my teeth in a way that might be mistaken for a smile. I turn and walk deeper into the building.

Here it is: on the back page of Section C, in a newspaper almost two weeks old. Didn't even make it to the airwaves, I guess. What difference does one more battered Asian make, after all the gang warfare going down in Chinatown? No wonder I missed it.

He had a name. Wai Chan. Found unconscious at a North Van housing development owned by Balthree Properties, where he was—

(Balthree Properties? They're local, aren't they?)

—where he was employed as a night watchman. In stable condition after being attacked by an unknown assailant. No motive. No suspects.

Bullshit. Half the fucking *city* is suspect, we've *all* got motive, and they know it.

Or maybe they don't. Maybe they believe all the stories they feed us that say Hey, High-Density Living Good For You, Crime Rate Unconnected To Population Size, Massive Immigration Keeps Us Safe From America, hurrah hurrah! Nothing like giving yourself a mild case of cancer to cure the measles, and every time somebody projects that the lower mainland will be sixty percent Chinese by 2010 the news is buried in a wave of stories about international goodwill and the cultural mosaic. Maybe they don't know what it's like to go back to the place you grew up and find it ripped to the ground, some off-shore conglomerate's turned it into another hive crammed with pulsing yellow grubs, perhaps Balthree Properties *isn't* run out of Hong Kong after all but I didn't know that *then*, did I? That used to be my *home*, there were trees there once, and childhood friends, and now just mud and lumber and this ugly little Chink yammering at me, barely even speaks the fucking language and he's *kicking me out of my own back yard*—

Once I felt guilty about what I did to him. I was sick with remorse. That was stupid, woolly thinking. My guilt doesn't spring from the one time I let the monster out. No sirree.

It springs from all the other times I didn't.

The Indians are on the warpath. From the endowment lands on east, they're blocking us. We're on their land, they say. They want justice. They want retribution. They want autonomy.

Don't tell me, noble savage. So do I.

Traffic moves nose-to-bumper like a procession of slugs. At this rate it'll be hours before I even get out of town, let alone home. There was a time when I could afford to live *in* town. There was even a time when I wanted to. Now, all I want to do is scream.

There's a group of Indian kids at the roadside, enjoying the chaos their parents have wrought. I bear them no ill will; the natives are a conquered people, drunk and unemployed, no threat to anyone. I sympathise. I honk my horn in support.

Thunk! A spiderweb explodes across my windshield, glassy cracks dividing and redividing into a network too fine to for my eyes to follow, I can barely see through—

Jesus! That sonofabitch threw a rock at me! There he is, winding up for another — no, he's after someone else this time, our ancestors weren't nice to their ancestors and this brat thinks that gives him some god-given moral right to trash other people's property—

I don't have to take this. *I* didn't take their fucking land away from them. Get off to the side, onto the shoulder — now floor it! Watch the skid, watch the skid — and look at those punks scrambling out of the way! One of them isn't quite fast enough; catches my eye as he rolls off the hood, and holy *shit* did his sneer vanish in a hurry! I do believe he already regrets the rashness of his actions, and we've barely started dancing yet.

I turn off the ignition. I pocket the keys.

I get out of the car.

There are people shouting somewhere very far away, and horns honking. They sound almost the same. Someone gets up off the pavement in front of me, nursing his leg. He doesn't look so tough now, does he? Like it's just dawned on him that they lost Oka years ago. Where did all your friends go, fucker? Where's Lasagna when you need him?

Okay, you want to wail about oppression? I'll show you oppression, you greasy Indian brat. I'm going to teach you a lesson you won't *ever* forget.

My muscles are knotted so tightly I wonder why my own ligaments haven't been torn out at the roots. I'm dimly aware that this is more or less normal for me now.

But I know that I'll feel better soon.

The Second Coming
of Jasmine Fitzgerald

What's wrong with this picture?

Not much, at first glance. Blood pools in a pattern entirely consistent with the location of the victim. No conspicuous arterial spray; the butchery's all abdominal, more spilled than spurted. No slogans either. Nobody's scrawled *Helter Skelter* or *Satan is Lord* or even *Elvis Lives* on any of the walls. It's just another mess in another kitchen in another one-bedroom apartment, already overcrowded with the piecemeal accumulation of two lives. One life's all that's left now, a thrashing gory creature screaming her mantra over and over as the police wrestle her away—

"I have to *save* him I have to *save* him I have to *save* him—"

—more evidence, not that the assembled cops need it, of why domestic calls absolutely *suck*.

She hasn't saved him. By now it's obvious that no one can. He lies in a pool of his own insides, blood and lymph spreading along the cracks between the linoleum tiles, crossing, criss-crossing, a convenient clotting grid drawing itself across the crime scene. Every now and then a red bubble grows and breaks on his lips. Anyone who happens to notice this, pretends not to.

The weapon? Right here: run-of-the-mill steak knife, slick with blood and coagulating fingerprints, lying exactly where she dropped it.

The only thing that's missing is a motive. They were a quiet couple, the neighbours say. He was sick, he'd been sick for months. They never went out much. There was no history of violence. They loved each other deeply.

Maybe she was sick too. Maybe she was following orders from some tumour in her brain. Or maybe it was a botched alien abduction, grey-skinned creatures from Zeta II Reticuli framing an innocent bystander for their own incompetence. Maybe it's a mass hallucination, maybe it isn't really happening at all.

Maybe it's an act of God.

They got to her early. This is one of the advantages of killing someone during office hours. They've taken samples, scraped residue from clothes and skin on the off chance that anyone might question whose blood she was wearing. They've searched the apartment, questioned neighbours and relatives, established the superficial details of identity: Jasmine Fitzgerald, 24-year-old Caucasian brunette, doctoral candidate. In Global General Relativity, whatever the fuck *that* is. They've stripped her down, cleaned her up, bounced her off a judge into Interview Room 1, Forensic Psychiatric Support Services.

They've put someone in there with her.

"Hello, Ms. Fitzgerald. I'm Dr. Thomas. My first name's Myles, if you prefer."

She stares at him. "Myles it is." She seems calm, but the tracks of recent tears still show on her face. "I guess you're supposed to decide whether I'm crazy."

"Whether you're fit to stand trial, yes. I should tell you right off that nothing you say to me is necessarily confidential. Do you understand?" She nods. Thomas sits down across from her. "What would you like me to call you?"

"Napoleon. Mohammed. Jesus Christ." Her lips twitch, the faintest smile, gone in an instant. "Sorry. Just kidding. Jaz's fine."

"Are you doing okay in here? Are they treating you all right?"

She snorts. "They're treating me pretty damn well, considering the kind of monster they think I am." A pause, then, "I'm not, you know."

"A monster?"

"Crazy. I've — I've just recently undergone a paradigm shift, you know? The whole world looks different, and my head's there but sometimes my gut — I mean, it's so hard to *feel* differently about things …"

"Tell me about this paradigm shift," Thomas suggests. He makes it a point not to take notes. He doesn't even have a notepad. Not that it matters. The microcassette recorder in his blazer has very sensitive ears.

"Things make sense now," she says. "They never did before. I think, for the first time in my life, I'm actually happy." She smiles again, for longer this time. Long enough for Thomas to marvel at how genuine it seems.

"You weren't very happy when you first came here," he says gently. "They say you were very upset."

"Yeah." She nods, seriously. "It's tough enough to do that shit to yourself, you know, but to risk someone else, someone you really care about—" She wipes at one eye. "He was dying for over a year, did you know that? Each day he'd hurt a little more. You could almost see it spreading through him, like some sort of — leaf, going brown. Or maybe that was the chemo. Never could decide which was worse." She shakes her head. "Heh. At least *that's* over now."

"Is that why you did it? To end his suffering?" Thomas doubts it. Mercy killers don't generally disembowel their beneficiaries. Still, he asks.

She answers. "Of course I fucked up, I only ended up making things worse." She clasps her hands in front of her. "I miss him already. Isn't that crazy? It only happened a few hours ago, and I know it's no big deal, but I still miss him. That head-heart thing again."

"You say you fucked up," Thomas says.

She takes a deep breath, nods. "Big time."

"Tell me about that."

"I don't know shit about debugging. I thought I did, but when you're dealing with organics — all I really did was go in and mess randomly with the code. You make a mess of everything, unless you know exactly what you're doing. That's what I'm working on now."

"Debugging?"

"That's what I call it. There's no real word for it yet."

Oh yes there is. Aloud: "Go on."

Jasmine Fitzgerald sighs, her eyes closed. "I don't expect you to believe this under the circumstances, but I really loved him. No: I *love* him." Her breath comes out in a soft snort, a whispered laugh. "There I go again. That bloody past tense."

"Tell me about debugging."

"I don't think you're up for it, Myles. I don't even think you're all that interested." Her eyes open, point directly at him. "But for the record, Stu was dying. I tried to save him. I failed. Next time I'll do better, and better still the time after that, and eventually I'll get it right."

"And what happens then?" Thomas says.

"Through your eyes or mine?"

"Yours."

"I repair the glitches in the string. Or if it's easier, I replicate an undamaged version of the subroutine and insert it back into the main loop. Same difference."

"Uh huh. And what would *I* see?"

She shrugs. "Stu rising from the dead."

What's wrong with this picture?

Spread out across the table, the mind of Jasmine Fitzgerald winks back from pages of standardised questions. Somewhere in here, presumably, is a monster.

These are the tools used to dissect human psyches. The WAIS. The MMPI. The PDI. Hammers, all of them. Blunt chisels posing as microtomes. A copy of the DSM-IV sits off to one side, a fat paperback volume of symptoms and pathologies. A matrix of pigeonholes. Perhaps Fitzgerald fits into one of them. Intermittent Explosive, maybe? Battered Woman? Garden-variety Sociopath?

The test results are inconclusive. It's as though she's laughing up from the page at him. *True or false: I sometimes hear voices that no one else hears.* False, she's checked. *I have been feeling unusually depressed lately.* False. *Sometimes I get so angry I feel like hitting something.* True, and a hand-written note in the margin: Hey, doesn't everyone?

There are snares sprinkled throughout these tests, linked questions designed to catch liars in subtle traps of self-contradiction. Jasmine Fitzgerald has avoided them all. Is she unusually honest? Is she too smart for the tests? There doesn't seem to be anything here that—

Wait a second.

Who was Louis Pasteur? asks the WAIS, trying to get a handle on educational background.

A virus, Fitzgerald said.

Back up the list. Here's another one, on the previous page: *Who was Winston Churchill?* And again: a virus.

And fifteen questions before *that*: *Who was Florence Nightingale?*

A famous nurse, Fitzgerald responded to that one. And her responses to all previous questions on historical personalities are unremarkably correct. But everyone after Nightingale is a virus.

Killing a virus is no sin. You can do it with an utterly clear conscience. Maybe she's redefining the nature of her act. Maybe that's how she manages to live with herself these days.

Just as well. That raising-the-dead shtick didn't cut any ice at all.

She's slumped across the table when he enters, her head resting on folded arms. Thomas clears his throat. "Jasmine."

No response. He reaches out, touches her lightly on the shoulder. Her head comes up, a fluid motion containing no hint of grogginess. She settles back into her chair and smiles. "Welcome back. So, am I crazy or what?"

Thomas smiles back and sits down across from her. "We try to avoid prejudicial terms."

"Hey, I can take it. I'm not prone to tantrums."

A picture flashes across the front of his mind: beloved husband, entrails spread-eagled like butterfly wings against a linoleum grid. *Of course not. No tantrums for you. We need a whole new word to describe what it is* you *do.*

'Debugging', wasn't it?

"I was going over your test results," he begins.

"Did I pass?"

"It's not that kind of test. But I was intrigued by some of your answers."

She purses her lips. "Good."

"Tell me about viruses."

That sunny smile again. "Sure. Mutable information strings that can't replicate without hijacking external source code."

"Go on."

"Ever hear of Core Wars?"

"No."

"Back in the early eighties some guys got together and wrote a bunch of self-replicating computer programs. The idea was to put them into the same block of memory and have them compete for space. They all had their own little tricks for self-defence and reproduction and, of course, eating the competition."

"Oh, you mean *computer* viruses," Thomas says.

"Actually, before all that." Fitzgerald pauses a moment, cocks her head to one side. "You ever wonder what it might be like to *be* one of those little programs? Running around laying eggs and dropping logic bombs and interacting with other viruses?"

Thomas shrugs. "I never even knew about them until now. Why? Do you?"

"No," she says. "Not any more."

"Go on."

Her expression changes. "You know, talking to *you* is a bit like talking a program. All you ever say is *go on* and *tell me more* and — I mean, Jesus, Myles, they wrote therapy programs back in the *sixties* that had more range than you do! In BASIC even! Register an *opinion*, for Chrissake!"

"It's just a technique, Jaz. I'm not here to get into a debate with you, as interesting as that might be. I'm trying to assess your fitness to stand trial. *My* opinions aren't really at issue."

She sighs, and sags. "I know. I'm sorry, I know you're not here to keep me entertained, but I'm *used* to being able to—

"I mean, *Stuart* would always be so—

"Oh, God. I miss him so *much*," she admits, her eyes shining and unhappy.

She's a killer, he tells himself. *Don't let her suck you in. Just assess her, that's all you have to do.*

Don't start liking her, for Christ's sake.

"That's — understandable," Thomas says.

She snorts. "Bullshit. You don't understand at all. You know what he did, the first time he went in for chemo? I was studying for my comps, and he stole my textbooks."

"Why would he do that?"

"Because he knew I wasn't studying at home. I was a complete wreck. And when I came to see him at the hospital he pulls these bloody books out from under his bed and starts quizzing me on Dirac and the Beckenstein Bound. He was *dying*, and all he wanted to do was help me prepare for some stupid test. I'd do anything for him."

Well, Thomas doesn't say, *You certainly did more than most.*

"I can't wait to see him again," she adds, almost as an afterthought.

"When will that be, Jaz?"

"When do you think?" She looks at him, and the sorrow and despair he thought he saw in those eyes is suddenly nowhere to be seen.

"Most people, if they said that, would be talking about the afterlife."

She favours him with a sad little smile. "This *is* the afterlife, Myles. This is Heaven, and Hell, and Nirvana. Whatever we choose to make it. Right here."

"Yes," Thomas says after a moment. "Of course."

Her disappointment in him hangs there like an accusation.

"You don't believe in God, do you?" she asks at last.

"Do you?" he ricochets.

"Didn't used to. Turns out there's clues, though. Proof, even."

"Such as?"

"The mass of the top quark. The width of the Higgs boson. You can't read them any other way when you know what you're looking for. Know anything about quantum physics, Myles?"

He shakes his head. "Not really."

"Nothing really exists, not down at the subatomic level. It's all just probability waves. Until someone looks at it, that is. Then the wave collapses and you get what we call *reality*. But it can't happen without an observer to get things started."

Thomas squints, trying to squeeze some sort of insight into his brain. "So if we weren't here looking at this table, it wouldn't exist?"

Fitzgerald nods. "More or less." That smile peeks around the corner of her mouth for a second.

He tries to lure it back. "So God's the observer, is that what you're saying? God watches all the atoms so the universe can exist?"

"Huh. I never thought about it that way before." The smile morphs into a frown of concentration. "More metaphoric than mathematical, but it's a cool idea."

"Was God watching you yesterday?"

She looks up, distracted. "Huh?"

"Does He — does It communicate with you?"

Her face goes completely expressionless. "Does God tell me to do things, you mean. Did God tell me to carve Stu up like — like—" Her breath hisses out between her teeth. "No, Myles. I don't hear voices. Charlie Manson doesn't come to me in my dreams and whisper sweet nothings. I answered all those questions on your test already, so give me a fucking break, okay?"

He holds up his hands, placating. "That's not what I meant, Jasmine." *Liar.* "I'm sorry if that's how it sounded, it's just — you know, God, quantum mechanics — it's a lot to swallow at once, you know? It's — mind-blowing."

She watches him through guarded eyes. "Yeah. I guess it can be. I forget, sometimes." She relaxes a fraction. "But it's all true. The math is inevitable. You can change the nature of reality, just by *looking* at it. You're right. It's mind-blowing."

"But only at the subatomic level, right? You're not *really* saying we could make this table disappear just by ignoring it, are you?"

Her eye flickers to a spot just to the right and behind him, about where the door should be.

"Well, no," she says at last. "Not without a lot of practise."

What's wrong with this picture?

Besides the obvious, of course. Besides the vertical incision running from sternum to approximately two centimetres below the navel, penetrating the abdominal musculature and extending through into the visceral coelom. Beyond the serrations along its edge which suggest the use of some sort of blade. Not, evidently, a very sharp one.

No. We're getting ahead of ourselves here. The coroner's art is nothing if not systematic. Very well, then: Caucasian male, mid-twenties. External morphometrics previously noted. Hair loss and bruising consistent with chemotherapeutic toxicity. Right index and ring fingernails missing, same notation. The deceased was one sick puppy at time of demise. Sickened by the disease, poisoned by the cure. And just when you thought things couldn't get any worse …

Down and in. The wound swallows the coroner's rubberised hands like some huge torn vagina, its labia clotted and crystallised. The usual viscera glisten inside, repackaged by medics at the site who had to reel in all loose ends for transport. Perhaps evidence was lost in the process. Perhaps the killer had arranged the entrails in some significant pattern, perhaps the arrangement of the GI tract spelled out some clue or unholy name. No matter. They took pictures of everything.

Mesentary stretches like thin latex, binding loops of intestine one to the other. A bit too tightly, in fact. There appear to be — fistulas of some sort, scattered along the lower ileum. Loops seem fused together at several spots. What could have caused that?

Nothing comes to mind.

Note it, record it, take a sample for detailed histological analysis. Move on. The scalpel passes through the tract as easily as through overcooked pasta. Stringy bile and pre-fecal lumps slump tiredly into a collecting dish. Something bulges behind them from the dorsal wall. Something shines white as bone where no bone should be. Slice, resect. There. A mass of some kind covering the right kidney, approximately fifteen centimetres by ten, extending down to the bladder. Quite heterogeneous, it's got some sort of *lumps* in it. A tumour? Is this what Stuart MacLennan's doctors were duelling with when they pumped him full of poison? It doesn't look like any tumour the coroner's seen.

For one thing — and this is really kind of strange — it's looking *back* at him.

His desk is absolutely spartan. Not a shred of paper out of place. Not a shred of paper even in evidence, actually. The surface is as featureless as a Kubrick monolith, except for the Sun workstation positioned dead centre and a rack of CDs angled off to the left.

"I *thought* she looked familiar," he says. "When I saw the papers. Didn't know quite where to place her, though."

Jasmine Fitzgerald's graduate supervisor.

"I guess you've got a lot of students," Thomas suggests.

"Yes." He leans forward, begins tapping at the workstation keyboard. "I've yet to meet all of them, actually. One or two in Europe I correspond with exclusively over the net. I hope to meet them this summer in Berne — ah, yes. Here she is; doesn't look anything like the media picture."

"She doesn't live in Europe, Dr. Russell."

"No, right here. Did her field work at CERN, though. Damn hard getting anything done here since the supercollider fell through. Ah."

"What?"

"She's on leave. I remember her now. She put her thesis on hold about a year and a half ago. Illness in the family, as I recall." Russell stares at the monitor; something he sees there seems to sink in, all at once.

"She killed her husband? She *killed* him?"

Thomas nods.

"My God." Russell shakes his head. "She didn't seem the type. She always seemed so — well, so cheery."

"She still does, sometimes."

"My God," he repeats. "And how can I help you?"

"She's suffering from some very elaborate delusions. She couches them in a lot of technical terminology I don't understand. I mean, for all I know she could actually be making *sense* — no, no. Scratch that. She *can't* be, but I don't have the background to really understand her, well, *claims*."

"What sort of *claims*?"

"For one thing, she keeps talking about bringing her husband back from the dead."

"I see."

"You don't seem surprised."

"Should I be? You said she was delusional."

Thomas takes a deep breath. "Dr. Russell, I've been doing

some reading the past couple of days. Popular cosmology, quantum mechanics for beginners, that sort of thing."

Russell smiles indulgently. "I suppose it's never too late to start."

"I get the impression that a lot of the stuff that happens down at the subatomic level almost has quasi-religious overtones. Spontaneous appearance of matter, simultaneous existence in different states. Almost spiritual."

"Yes, I suppose that's true. After a fashion."

"Are cosmologists a religious lot, by and large?"

"Not really." Russell drums fingers on his monolith. "The field's so strange that we don't really *need* religious experience on top of it. Some of the eastern religions make claims that sound vaguely quantum-mechanical, but the similarities are pretty superficial."

"Nothing more, well, Christian? Nothing that would lead someone to believe in a single omniscient God who raises the dead?"

"God no. Oh, except for that Tipler fellow." Russell leans forward. "Why? Jasmine Fitzgerald hasn't become a Christian, has she?" Murder is one thing, his tone suggests, but *this* …

"I don't think so," Thomas reassures him. "Not unless Christianity's broadened its tenets to embrace human sacrifice."

"Yes. Quite." Russell leans back again, apparently satisfied.

"Who's Tipler?" Thomas asks.

"Mmmm?" Russell blinks, momentarily distracted. "Oh, yes. Frank Tipler. Cosmologist from Tulane, claimed to have a testable mathematical proof of the existence of God. And the afterlife too, if I recall. Raised a bit of a stir a few years back."

"I take it you weren't impressed."

"Actually, I didn't follow it very closely. Theology's not that interesting to me. I mean, if physics proves that there is or there isn't a God that's fine, but that's not really the point of the exercise, is it?"

"I couldn't say. Seems to me it'd be a hell of a spin-off, though." Russell smiles.

"I don't suppose you've got the reference?" Thomas suggests.

"Of course. Just a moment." Russell feeds a CD to the workstation and massages the keyboard. The Sun purrs. "Yes, here it is: *The Physics of Immortality: Modern Cosmology, God and the*

Resurrection of the Dead. 1994, Frank J. Tipler. I can print you out the complete citation if you want."

"Please. So what was his proof?"

The professor displays something akin to a very small smile.

"In thirty words or less," Thomas adds. "For idiots."

"Well," Russell says, "basically, he argued that some billions of years hence, life will incorporate itself into a massive quantum-effect computing device to avoid extinction when the universe collapses."

"I thought the universe wasn't *going* to collapse," Thomas interjects. "I thought they proved it was just going to keep expanding ..."

"That was last year," Russell says shortly. "May I continue?"

"Yes, of course."

"Thank you. As I was saying, Tipler claimed that billions of years hence, life will incorporate itself into a massive quantum-effect computing device to avoid extinction when the universe collapses. An integral part of this process involves the exact reproduction of everything that ever happened in the universe up to that point, right down to the quantum level, as well as all possible variations of those events."

Beside the desk, Russell's printer extrudes a paper tongue. He pulls it free and hands it over.

"So God's a supercomputer at the end of time? And we'll all be resurrected in the mother of all simulation models?"

"Well—" Russell wavers. The caricature seems to cause him physical pain. "I suppose so," he finishes, reluctantly. "In thirty words or less, as you say."

"Wow." Suddenly Fitzgerald' ravings sound downright pedestrian. "But if he's right—"

"The consensus is he's not," Russell interjects hastily.

"But *if*. If the model's an exact reproduction, how could you tell the difference between real life and afterlife? I mean, what would be the *point*?"

"Well, the point is avoiding ultimate extinction, supposedly. As to how you'd tell the difference ..." Russell shakes his head. "Actually, I never finished the book. As I said, theology doesn't interest me all that much."

Thomas shakes his head. "I can't believe it."

"Not many could," Russell says. Then, almost apologetically, he adds "Tipler's theoretical proofs were quite extensive, though, as I recall."

"I bet. Whatever happened to him?"

Russell shrugs. "What happens to anyone who's stupid enough to come up with a new way of looking at the world? They tore into him like sharks at a feeding frenzy. I don't know where he ended up."

What's wrong with this picture?

Nothing. Everything. Suddenly awake, Myles Thomas stares around a darkened studio and tries to convince himself that nothing has changed.

Nothing *has* changed. The faint sounds of late-night traffic sound the same as ever. Grey parallelograms stretch across wall and ceiling, a faint luminous shadow of his bedroom window cast by some distant streetlight. Natalie's still gone from the left side of his bed, her departure so far removed by now that he doesn't even have to remind himself of it.

He checks the LEDs on his bedside alarm: 2:35a.m.

Something's different.

Nothing's changed.

Well, maybe one thing. Tipler's heresy sits on the night stand, its plastic dustcover reflecting slashes of red light from the alarm clock. *The Physics of Immortality: Modern Cosmology, God and the Resurrection of the Dead.* It's too dark to read the lettering but you don't forget a title like that. Myles Thomas signed it out of the library this afternoon, opened it at random

… Lemma 1, and the fact that f_{ij} $\sum_{k\ 1} f_{ij}^{(k)}$ 1 , we have

$$\sum_{n\ 1} p_{ij}^{(n)} \qquad \sum_{n\ 1}\sum_{k\ 1}^{n} f_{ij}^{(k)} p_{jj}^{(n\ k)} \qquad \sum_{k\ 1} f_{ij}^{(k)} \sum_{n\ 0} p_{jj}^{(n)}$$

$$f_{ij} \sum_{n\ 0} p_{ij}^{(n)} \qquad \sum_{n\ 0} p_{jj}^{(n)}$$

which is just (*E*.3), and (*E*.3) can hold only if …

and threw it into his briefcase, confused and disgusted. He doesn't even know why he went to the effort of getting the fucking thing. Jasmine Fitzgerald is delusional. It's that simple. For reasons that it is not Myles Thomas' job to understand, she vivisected her husband on the kichen floor. Now she's inventing all sorts of ways to excuse herself, to undo the undoable, and the fact that she cloaks her delusions in cosmological gobbledegook does not make them any more credible. What does he expect to do, turn into a quantum mechanic overnight? Is he going to learn even a fraction of what he'd need to find the holes in her carefully constructed fantasy? Why did he even bother?

But he did. And now *Modern Cosmology, God and the Resurrection of the Dead* looms dimly in front of him at two thirty in the fucking morning, and something's changed, he's almost *sure* of it, but try as he might he can't get a handle on what it is. He just feels different, somehow. He just feels …

Awake. That's what you feel. You couldn't get back to sleep now if your life depended on it.

Myles Thomas sighs and turns on the reading lamp. Squinting as his pupils shrink against the light, he reaches out and grabs the offending book.

Parts of it, astonishingly, almost make sense.

"She's not here," the orderly tells him. "Last night we had to move her next door."

Next door: the hospital. "Why? What's wrong?"

"Not a clue. Convulsions, cyanosis — we thought she was toast, actually. But by the time the doctor got to her she couldn't find anything wrong."

"That doesn't make any sense."

"Tell me about it. Nothing about that crazy b — nothing about her makes sense." The orderly wanders off down the hall, frowning.

Jasmine Fitzgerald lies between sheets tucked tight as a straitjacket, stares unblinking at the ceiling. A nurse sits to one side, boredom and curiosity mixing in equal measures on his face.

"How is she?" Thomas asks.

"Don't really know," the nurse says. "She seems okay now."

"She doesn't look okay to me. She looks almost catatonic."

"She isn't. Are you, Jaz?"

"We're sorry," Fitzgerald says cheerfully. "The person you are trying to reach is temporarily unavailable. Please leave a message and we'll get back to you." Then: "Hi, Myles. Good to see you." Her eyes never waver from the acoustic tiles overhead.

"You better blink one of these days," Thomas remarks. "Your eyeballs are going to dry up."

"Nothing a little judicious editing won't fix," she tells him.

Thomas glances at the nurse. "Would you excuse us for a few minutes?"

"Sure. I'll be in the caf if you need me."

Thomas waits until the door swings shut. "So, Jaz. What's the mass of the Higgs boson?"

She blinks.

She smiles.

She turns to look at him.

"Two hundred twenty eight GeV," she says. "All *right*. Someone actually *read* my thesis proposal."

"Not just your proposal. That's one of Tipler's testable predictions, isn't it?"

Her smile widens. "The critical one, actually. The others are pretty self-evident."

"And you tested it."

"Yup. Over at CERN. So how'd you find his book?"

"I only read parts of it," Thomas admits. "It was pretty tough slogging."

"Sorry. My fault," Fitzgerald says.

"How so?"

"I thought you could use some help, so I souped you up a bit. Increased your processing speed. Not enough, I guess."

Something shivers down his back. He ignores it.

"I'm not—" Thomas rubs his chin; he forgot to shave this morning "—exactly sure what you mean by that."

"Sure you do. You just don't believe it." Fitzgerald squirms up from between the sheets, props her back against a pillow. "It's just a semantic difference, Myles. You'd call it a *delusion*. Us physics geeks would call it a *hypothesis*."

Thomas nods, uncertainly.

"Oh, just say it, Myles. I know you're dying to."

"Go on," he blurts, strangely unable to stop himself.

Fitzgerald laughs. "If you insist, Doctor. I figured out what I was doing wrong. I thought I had to do everything myself, and I just can't. Too many variables, you see, even if you access them individually there's no way you can keep track of 'em all at once. When I tried, I got mixed up and everything—"

A sudden darkness in her face now. A memory, perhaps, pushing up through all those careful layers of contrivance.

"Everything went wrong," she finishes softly.

Thomas nods, keeps his voice low and gentle. "What are you remembering right now, Jaz?"

"You know damn well what I'm remembering," she whispers. "I — I cut him open—"

"Yes."

"He was dying. He was *dying*. I tried to fix him, I tried to fix the code but something went wrong, and ..."

He waits. The silence stretches.

"... and I didn't know what. I couldn't fix it if I couldn't see what I'd done wrong. So I — I cut him open ..." Her brow furrows suddenly. Thomas can't tell with what: remembrance, remorse?

"I really overstepped myself," she says at last.

No. Concentration. She's rebuilding her defences, she's pushing the tip of that bloody iceberg back below the surface. It can't be easy. Thomas can see it, ponderous and massively buoyant, pushing up from the depths while Jasmine Fitzgerald leans down and desperately pretends not to strain.

"I know it must be difficult to think about," Thomas says.

She shrugs. "Sometimes." *Going* ... "When my head slips back into the old school. Old habits die hard." *Going* ... "But I get over it."

The frown disappears.

Gone.

"You know when I told you about Core Wars?" she asks brightly.

After a moment, Thomas nods.

"All viruses replicate, but some of the better ones can write macros — *micros*, actually, would be a better name for them — to other addresses, little subroutines that autonomously perform simple tasks. And some of *those* can replicate too. Get my drift?"

"Not really," Thomas says quietly.

"I really should have souped you up a bit more. Anyway, those little routines, they can handle all the book-keeping. Each one tracks a few variables, and each time they replicate that's a few more, and pretty soon there's no limit to the size of the problem you can handle. Hell, you could rewrite the whole damn operating system from the inside out and not have to worry about any of the details, all your little daemons are doing that for you."

"Are we all just viruses to you, Jaz?"

She laughs at that, not unkindly. "Ah, Myles. It's a technical term, not a moral judgement. Life's information, shaped by natural selection. That's all I mean."

"And you've learned to — rewrite the code," Thomas says.

She shakes her head. "Still learning. But I'm getting better at it all the time."

"I see." Thomas pretends to check his watch. He still doesn't know the jargon. He never will. But at least, at last, he knows where she's coming from.

Nothing left but the final platitudes.

"That's all I need right now, Jasmine. I want to thank you for being so co-operative. I know how tough this must be on you."

She cocks her head at him, smiling. "This is goodbye then, Myles? You haven't come *close* to curing me."

He smiles back. He can almost feel each muscle fibre contracting, the increased tension on facial tendons, soft tissue stretching over bone. The utter insincerity of a purely mechanical process. "That's not what I'm here for, Jaz."

"Right. You're assessing my fitness."

Thomas nods.

"Well?" she asks after a moment. "Am I fit?"

He takes a breath. "I think you have some problems you haven't faced. But you can understand counsel, and there's no doubt you could follow any proceedings the court is likely to throw at you. Legally, that means you can stand trial."

"Ah. So I'm not sane, but I'm not crazy enough to get off, eh?"

"I hope things work out for you." That much, at least, is sincere.

"Oh, they will," she says easily. "Never fear. How much longer do I stay here?"

"Maybe another three weeks. Thirty days is the usual period."

"But you've finished with me. Why so long?"

He shrugs. "Nowhere else to put you, for now."

"Oh." She considers. "Just as well, I guess. It'll given me more time to practice."

"Goodbye, Jasmine."

"Too bad you missed Stuart," she says behind him. "You'd have liked him. Maybe I'll bring him around to your place sometime."

The doorknob sticks. He tries again.

"Something wrong?" she asks.

"No," Thomas says, a bit too quickly. "It's just—"

"Oh, right. Hang on a sec." She rustles in her sheets.

He turns his head. Jasmine Fitzgerald lies flat on her back, unblinking, staring straight up. Her breath is fast and shallow.

The doorknob seems subtly warmer in his hand.

He releases it. "Are you okay?"

"Sure," she says to the ceiling. "Just tired. Takes a bit out of you, you know?"

Call the nurse, he thinks.

"Really, I just need some rest." She looks at him one last time, and giggles. "But Myles to go before I sleep …"

"Dr. Desjardins, please."

"Speaking."

"You performed the autopsy on Stuart MacLennan?"

A brief silence. Then: "Who is this?"

"My name's Myles Thomas. I'm a psychologist at FPSS. Jasmine Fitzgerald is — was a client of mine."

The phone sits there in his hand, silent.

"I was looking at the case report, writing up my assessment, and I just noticed something about your findings—"

"They're preliminary," Desjardins interrupts. "I'll have the full report, um, shortly."

"Yes, I understand that, Dr. Desjardins. But my understanding is that MacLennan was, well, mortally wounded."

"He was gutted like a fish," Desjardins says.

"Right. But your r — your *preliminary* report lists cause of death as 'undetermined'."

"That's because I haven't determined the cause of death."

"Right. I guess I'm a bit confused about what else it could have been. You didn't find any toxins in the body, at least none that weren't involved in MacLennan's chemo, and no other injuries except for these fistulas and teratomas—"

The phone barks in Thomas's hand, a short ugly laugh. "Do you know what a teratoma *is*?" Desjardins asks.

"I assumed it was something to do with his cancer."

"Ever hear the term *primordial cyst*?"

"No."

"Hope you haven't eaten recently," Desjardins says. "Every now and then you get a clump of proliferating cells floating around in the coelomic cavity. Something happens to activate the dormant genes — could be a lot of things, but the upshot is you sometimes get these growing blobs of tissue sprouting teeth and hair and bone. Sometimes they get as big as grapefruits."

"My God. MacLennan had one of those in him?"

"I thought, maybe. At first. Turned out to be a chunk of his kidney. Only there was an eye growing out of it. And most of his abdominal lymph nodes, too, the ducts were clotted with hair and something like fingernail. It was keratinised, anyway."

"That's horrible," Thomas whispers.

"No shit. Not to mention the perforated diaphragm, or the fact that half the loops of his small intestine were fused together."

"But I thought he had leukaemia."

"He did. That wasn't what killed him."

"So you're saying these teratomas might have had some role in MacLennan's death?"

"I don't see how," Desjardins says.

"But—"

"Look, maybe I'm not making myself clear. I have my doubts that Stuart MacLennan died from his wife's carving skills because any *one* of the abnormalities I found should have killed him more or less instantly."

"But that's pretty much impossible, isn't it? I mean, what did the investigating officers say?"

"Quite frankly, I don't think they read my report," Desjardins grumbles. "Neither did you, apparently, or you would have called me before now."

"Well, it wasn't really central to my assessment, Dr. Desjardins. And besides, it seemed so obvious—"

"For sure. You see someone laid open from crotch to sternum, you don't need any report to know what killed him. Who cares about any of this congenital abnormality bullshit?"

Congen— "You're saying he was *born* that way?"

"Except he couldn't have been. He'd never have even made it to his first breath."

"So you're saying—"

"I'm saying Stuart MacLennan's wife couldn't have killed him, because physiologically there's no way in hell that he could have been alive to start with."

Thomas stares at the phone. It offers no retraction.

"But — he was twenty-eight years old! How could that be?"

"God only knows," Desjardins tells him. "You ask me, it's a fucking miracle."

What's wrong with this picture?

He isn't quite certain, because he doesn't quite know what he was expecting. No opened grave, no stone rolled dramatically away from the sepulchre. Of course not. Jasmine Fitzgerald would probably say that her powers are too subtle for such obvious theatre. Why leave a pile of shovelled earth, an opened coffin, when you can just rewrite the code?

She sits cross-legged on her husband's undisturbed grave. Whatever powers she lays claim to, they don't shield her from the light rain falling on her head. She doesn't even have an umbrella.

"Myles," she says, not looking up. "I thought it might be you." Her sunny smile, that radiant expression of happy denial, is nowhere to be seen. Her face is as expressionless as her husband's must be, two meters down.

"Hello, Jaz," Thomas says.

"How did you find me?" she asks him.

"FPSS went ballistic when you disappeared. They're calling everyone who had any contact with you, trying to figure out how you got out. Where you might be."

Her fingers play in the fresh earth. "Did you tell them?"

"I didn't think of this place until after," he lies. Then, to atone: "And I don't *know* how you got out."

"Yes you do, Myles. You do it yourself all the time."

"Go on," he says, deliberately.

She smiles, but it doesn't last. "We got here the same way, Myles. We copied ourselves from one address to another. The only difference is, you still have to go from A to B to C. I just cut straight to Z. "

"I can't accept that," Thomas says.

"Ever the doubter, aren't you? How can you enjoy heaven when you can't even recognise it?" Finally, she looks up at him. "*You should be told the difference between empiricism and stubbornness, doctor.* Know what that's from?"

He shakes his head.

"Oh well. It's not important." She looks back at the ground. Wet tendrils of hair hang across her face. "They wouldn't let me come to the funeral."

"You don't seem to need their permission."

"Not now. That was a few days ago. I still hadn't worked all the bugs out then." She plunges one hand into wet dirt. "You know what I did to him."

Before the knife, she means.

"I'm not — I don't really—"

"You know," she says again.

Finally he nods, although she isn't looking.

The rain falls harder. Thomas shivers under his windbreaker. Fitzgerald doesn't seem to notice.

"So what now?" he asks at last.

"I'm not sure. It seemed so straightforward at first, you know? I loved Stuart, completely, without reservation. I was going to bring him back as soon as I learned how. I was going to do it right this time. And I still love him, I really do, but damn it all I don't love *everything* about him, you know? He was a slob, sometimes. And I hated his taste in music. So now that I'm here, I figure, why stop at just bringing him back? Why not, well, fine-tune him a bit?"

"Is that what you're going to do?"

"I don't know. I'm going through all the things I'd change, and when it comes right down to it maybe it'd be better to just start again from scratch. Less — intensive. Computationally."

"I hope you *are* delusional." Not a wise thing to say, but suddenly he doesn't care. "Because if you're not, God's a really callous bastard."

"Is it," she says, without much interest.

"Everything's just information. We're all just subroutines interacting in a model somewhere. Well nothing's really all that important then, is it? You'll get around to debugging Stuart one of these days. No hurry. He can wait. It's just microcode, nothing's irrevocable. So nothing really *matters*, does it? How could God give a shit about anything in a universe like that?"

Jasmine Fitzgerald rises from the grave and wipes the dirt off her hands. "Watch it, Myles." There's a faint smile on her face. "You don't want to piss me off."

He meets her eyes. "I'm glad I still can."

"*Touché.*" There's still a twinkle there, behind her soaked lashes and the runnels of rainwater coursing down her face.

"So what are you going to do?" he asks again.

She looks around the soaking graveyard. "Everything. I'm going to clean the place up. I'm going to fill in the holes. I'm going to rewrite Planck's constant so it makes *sense*." She smiles at him. "Right now, though, I think I'm just going to go somewhere and think about things for a while."

She steps off the mound. "Thanks for not telling on me. It wouldn't have made any difference, but I appreciate the thought. I won't forget it." She begins to walk away in the rain.

"Jaz," Thomas calls after her.

She shakes her head, without looking back. "Forget it, Myles. Nobody handed *me* any miracles." She stops, then, turns briefly.

"Besides, you're not ready. You'd probably just think I hypnotised you or something."

I should stop her, Thomas tells himself. *She's dangerous. She's deluded. They could charge me with aiding and abetting. I should stop her.*

If I can.

She leaves him in the rain with the memory of that bright, guiltless smile. He's almost sure he doesn't feel anything pass through him then. But maybe he does. Maybe it feels like a ripple growing across some stagnant surface. A subtle reweaving of electrons. A small change in the way things are.

I'm going to clean the place up. I'm going to fill in the holes.

Myles Thomas doesn't know exactly what she meant by that. But he's afraid that soon — far too soon — there won't be anything wrong with this picture.

Bulk Food

Laurie Channer & Peter Watts

Anna Marie Hamilton, Animal Rights Microstar, bastes in the media spotlight just outside the aquarium gates. Her followers hang on every movement, their placards rising and falling like cardboard whitecaps to the rhythm of their chant: *two, four, six, eight, Transients are what we hate*—

One whale-hugger, bedecked in a sandwich board reading *Eat the Transients*, shouts over the din at a nearby reporter: "Naw, it's not about the *homeless* — it's a *whale* thing, man ..."

The reporter isn't really listening. Anna Marie has just opened her mouth. The chanting dies instantly. It's always interesting to hear what Anna Marie Hamilton says. It changes so often, these days. Back before the Breakthrough, she was actually trying to *free* the whales. She was going around calling them *prisoners*, and *hostages*, for Christ's sake.

"*Save the whales ...*" she begins.

The reporter grunts, disappointed. *That again ...*

Over at the turnstiles, Doug Largha swipes his debit card and passes through. The protesters register vaguely on his radar. Back in his student days, he considered joining, but only with the hope of scoring with some of those touchy-feely whale chicks. The things he did, back then, to get laid.

Hell. The things he does *now* ...

A foghorn calls across the Strait. Visibility's low on both sides of the world; the murk is gray above the waterline, green below. The sea around Race Rocks is empty. This place used to be a wildlife sanctuary. Now it's a DMZ.

Two hundred meters out from the islands, perimeter sensors listen patiently for intruders. There are none. The day's too cold for tourists, too foggy for spies, too damn wet for most terrestrial mammals. Nobody tries to cross over the line. Even *under* the line, traffic is way down from the old days. An occasional trio of black-and-white teardrops, each the size of a school bus. Every now and then a knife-edged dorsal fin, tall as a man. Nothing else.

There was a lot more happening out here a few years ago. Race Rocks used to be crawling with seals, sea lions, Dall's porpoises. It was a regular Who's Who back then: *Eschrichtius, Phocoena, Zalophus, Eumetopias.*

All that meat has long since been cleaned out. Just one species comes through here these days: *Orcinus.* Nobody asks *these* visitors for ID. They've got their own way of doing things.

Five kilometers east, the commercial trawler *Dipnet* wallows forward at half throttle. Vague gray shapes crowd restlessly along the gunwales, slick, wet, hooded against the soupy atmosphere. Even a fog that drains all color from the world can't dampen the enthusiasm on board. Snatches of song drift across the waves, male and female voices in chorus.

"And they'll know we are sisters by our love, by our love …"

Twenty-five meters down, a string of clicks ratchets through the water column. It sounds like the drumming of impatient fingers.

Doug's got everything figured. He's found the perfect position; right next to the rim, where the gangway extends over the tank like a big fiberglass tongue. Other spectators, with less foresight or less motivation, fill the bleachers ringing the main tank. Plexi splashguards separate them from a million gallons of filtered seawater and the predatory behemoth within. On the far side of the tank, more fiberglass and a few tons of molded cement impersonate a rocky coastline. Every few moments a smooth black back rolls across the surface, its dorsal fin stiff as a horny penis. No floppy-fin syndrome *here*, no siree. This isn't the old days.

The show is due to start momentarily. Doug uses the time to go over the plan once more. Twenty seconds from tongue to gallery. Another thirty-five to the gift shop. Fifty-five seconds total, if he doesn't run into anyone. Perhaps sixty if he does. He'll beat them all. Doug Largha is a man on a mission.

A fanfare from the poolside speakers. A perky blonde emerges through a sudden hole in the coastal facade, wearing the traditional garb of the order: white shorts and a ducky blue staff shirt. An odd-looking piece of electronics hangs off her belt. A headset mike arcs across one cheek. The crowd cheers.

Behind the blonde, some Japanese guy hovers in the wings with an equally-Japanese kid of about twelve. The woman waves them on deck as she greets the audience.

"Good afternoon!" she chirps resoundingly over the speakers. "Welcome to the aquarium, and welcome to today's whale show!"

More applause.

"Our special guest today is Tetsuo Yamamoto, and his father, Herschel." The woman raises one arm over the water. "And our *other* special guest is, of course, *Shamu!*"

Doug snorts. They're *always* called Shamu. The Aquarium doesn't put much thought into naming killer whales these days.

"My name is Ramona, and I'll be your naturalist today." She waits for applause. There isn't much, but she acknowledges it like a standing ovation and goes into patter. "Now of course, we've been able to understand Orcan ever since The Breakthrough, but we still can't *speak* it — at least, not without some very expensive hardware to help us with the higher frequencies. Fortunately our state-of-the-art translation software, developed right here at the Aquarium, lets our species talk to each other. I'll be asking Shamu to do some behaviors especially so Tetsuo here can interact with him."

Figures the kid would be center stage. Probably some Japanese rite of passage. Number One Son looks like a typical clumsy thumb-fingered preadolescent. This could be the day.

"As you may have learned from our award-winning educational displays," Ramona continues brightly, "our coast is home to two different orca societies, *Residents* and *Transients*. Both societies are ruled by the oldest females — the Matriarchs — but beyond that they have don't have much in common. In fact, they actively hate each other."

A rhythmic stomping begins from somewhere in the crowd. Ramona cranks up the smile and the volume, and forges ahead. *Research and Education*: that's the aquarium's motto, and they're sticking to it. You don't get to the good stuff until you've *learned* something.

"Now we've known since the nineteen-seventies that Transients hunt seals, dolphins, even other whales, while the Residents feed only on fish. We didn't know why until after The Breakthrough, though. It turns out that Residents are the killer whale version of animal-rights activists!" This is obviously supposed to be a joke. Nobody's laughed at that line since Doug started casing this place over a year ago, but the song remains the same.

Unfazed, Ramona continues: "Yes, the Residents consider it *unethical* to eat other mammals. Transients, on the other hand, believe that their gods have given them the right to eat anything in the ocean. Each group regards the other as immoral, and Residents and Transients have not been on speaking terms for hundreds of years. Of course, we at the Aquarium haven't taken sides. *Most* humans know better than to interfere in the religious affairs of others."

Ramona pauses. A faint chant of assembled voices drifts into the silence from beyond the outer wall:

"Hey *ho* — hey *ho* — the *Ma*triarchs have *got* to *go*—"

Ramona smiles. "And despite what some people might think," she continues, "there's no such thing as a vegetarian orca."

Not yet, anyway.

Dipnet chugs steadily west. Her cargo of ambassadors scans the waves for any sign of the natives, their faith too strong to falter before anything so inconsequential as zero visibility. Not everyone gets to commune with an alien intelligence. A superior intelligence, in many ways.

Not in *every* way, of course. Many on the *Dipnet* long for the good old days of moral absolutes, the days when *Meat Was Murder* only when Humans ate it. Everything was so clear back then, to anyone who wasn't a puppet of the Industrial-Protein

Complex. There was a ready answer to anything the Ignorantsia might ask:

How come it's okay for sharks to kill baby seals? Because sharks aren't *moral agents*. They can't see the ethical implications of their actions.

How come it's not okay for people to kill baby seals? Because we *can*.

Now orcas are moral agents too. They talk. They think. They reason. Not that that's any surprise to *Dipnet*'s passengers, of course — they knew the truth way back when all those bozo scientists were insisting that orcas were basically chimps with fins. But sometimes, too much insight can lead to the wrong kind of questions, questions that distract one from the truth. Questions like:

How come it's okay for orcas to kill baby seals, but we can't?

If only those idiot scientists hadn't barged in and *proved* everything. Now there's no choice but to get the orcas to give up meat.

The Residents have the greatest moral potential. At least they draw the line at fish. The Transients remain relentlessly bull-headed in their mammalvory, but perhaps the Residents can be brought to full enlightenment. Back on shore, one of the west coast's best-known Kirlian nutritionists is working tirelessly on alternate ways to meet *Orcinus'* dietary requirements. She's already had some spectacular successes with her own cats. Not only is a vegan diet vastly more efficient than conventional pet foods — the cats eat only a fraction of what they used to — but the felines have so much more energy now that they're always out on the prowl. You hardly ever see them at home any more.

Not everything goes so well, of course. There've been setbacks. In hindsight, it may have been premature to dump that thousand heads of Romaine lettuce onto A4-Pod last summer during their spring migration. Not only did the Residents fail to convert to Veganism, but apparently they'd actually been considering certain exceptions to their eat-no-mammals policy. Fortunately, everyone on the boat had made it back okay.

But that's in the past. Live and learn. Today, it is enough to stand in solidarity with the Residents against the mammal-phagous Transient foe, to add Human voices in peaceful protest for a just cause. The moral education can come later. Now it is time to make friends.

The men and women of the *Dipnet* have the utmost faith in their abilities in this regard. They're ready, they're willing, they're the best of the best.

What else could they be? Every last one of them was hand-picked by Anna-Marie Hamilton.

Shamu sails past Doug in mid-air, his ivory belly a good two meters above water level. Their eyes meet. For all this talk about killer whale intelligence, it still looks like a big dumb fish to Doug.

It belly-flops. A small tsunami climbs the splashguards. A few scattered voices go *oooooh*.

"Now, Shamu is a Transient, so of course he'd *never* normally eat fish," Ramona announces. This is not entirely true. Back before the Breakthrough, fish was all captive Transients *ever* got. A decent meal plan was one of the first things they negotiated when the language barrier fell. "So to feed him what he *really* wants, he knows he has to *hide* for a bit."

Ramona touches a control on her belt and speaks into the mike. What's coming out of the speakers now isn't English. It sounds more like fingernails on a blackboard.

Shamu spits back a series of clicks and sinks below the surface. Waves surge back and forth across the tank, playing themselves out against the walls. Doug, standing on tiptoes, can just barely make out the black-and-white shape lurking near the bottom of the tank like a squad car at a radar trap.

Peripheral movement. Doug glances up as a great chocolate-colored shape lumbers out onto the deck. It's twice the size of the man who herds it onstage with a little help from an electric cattle prod.

"Some of you may recognize this big bruiser." Ramona's switched back to English. "Yes, this is a *Steller sea lion*. When he was just a pup, scientists from the North Pacific Fishing Consortium — one of the aquarium's proudest sponsors — rescued him and some of his friends from the wild. They were part of a research project that was intended to promote the conservation of sea lions in the North Pacific."

The sea lion darts its head back and forth, snorting like a horse. Its wet, brown eyes blink stupidly.

"And not a moment too soon. As you may know from our ever-popular Pinniped habitat, Stellers were declared extinct in the wild just five years ago. This is now one of the only places in the world where you can still see these magnificent creatures, and we take our responsibility to our charges very seriously. We go to great lengths to ensure that everything about their environment is as natural as possible.

"Including ..."

Ramona pauses for effect.

"... Predators."

A ragged cheer rises up from the bleachers. Spooked, the sea lion bobs its head like a fat furry metronome. The animal wheels around the way it came, but the guy with the prod is blocking its way.

"Please try not to make any loud noises or sudden moves," Ramona smiles belatedly.

With a few final nudges from the cattle prod, the sea lion slides into the water. It dives immediately, finally curious about its big new home.

Apparently it discovers all it wants to in about half a second, after which it shoots from the center of the pool like a Polaris missile. It doesn't quite achieve escape velocity and hits the water running, lunging for the edge as fast as its flippers can churn.

Shamu rises up like Shiva. One effortless chomp and the Steller explodes like a big wet piñata. A curtain of blood drenches the plexi barriers. Streamers of intestine fly through the air like shiny pink firehoses.

The audience goes wild. This is the kind of award-winning educational display they can relate to.

Shamu surges back and forth, mopping up leftover sea lion. It takes less than a minute. By the time he's finished, Ramona has the harpoon set up on the gangway.

Two kilometers out, one of the Chosen hears a blow and

alerts the others. The pilgrims again fall expectantly silent, undaunted by the fact that the first three times turned out to be the first mate blowing his nose.

To be honest, nobody here has ever heard a real orca blow, not first-hand. No *civilized* human being would ever patronize a whalejail, and whale-watching tours have been banned for years — they *said* it was a harassment issue, but everyone knows it was just Bob Finch and his aquarium industry cronies out to eliminate the competition.

The passengers huddle quietly in the fog, straining to hear above *Dipnet*'s diesel cough.

Whoosh.

"There! I knew it!" And sure enough, something rolls across a fog-free patch of surface a few meters to port. "There! See?"

Whoosh. Whoosh.

Two more to starboard. Leviathan has come to greet them; her very breath seems to dispel the fog. A pale patch of tissue-paper sun lightens the sky.

There is much rejoicing. One or two people close their eyes, choosing to commune with the orcas telepathically; no truly enlightened soul would resort to crass, earth-raping *technology* to make contact. Several others bring out dog-eared editions of Bigg's *Guide to the Genealogy and Natural History of Killer Whales*. Anna Marie has told them they'll be meeting L1, a southern Resident pod. Hungry eyes alternately scan the pages and the rolling black flanks for telltale nicks and markings.

"Look, is that L55? See that pointy bit on the saddle patch?"

"No, it's L2. Of course it's L2."

One of the telepaths speaks up. "You shouldn't call them by their Human names. They might find it offensive."

Chastened silence fall over the acolytes. After a moment, someone clears her throat. "Er, what *should* we call them then?"

The telepath looks about quickly. "Um, this one," she points to the fin nearest the boat, "tells me she's called, um, Sister Stargazer."

The others ooh in unison. Their hands fly to the crystals nestled beneath their rain ponchos.

"Six-foot dorsal," mutters the first mate. "Male."

No one notices. "Oh, look at that *big* one! I think that's the *Matriarch*!"

"Are you sure this is even L-Pod?" someone else asks uncertainly. "There aren't very many of them — isn't L1 supposed to be a *big* pod? And I thought I saw … that is, wasn't that big one P-28?"

That stops everyone cold. "P-28 is Transient," says a fortyish woman with periwinkle shells braided into her long, graying hair. "L1 is a *Resident* pod." The accusation is clear. Is this man calling Anna Marie Hamilton a *liar*?

The heretic falters in the stony silence. "Well, that's what the Guide says." He holds the document out like a protective amulet.

"Give me that." Periwinkle snatches the book away, riffles through the pages. "This is the *old* edition." She waves the copyright page. "This was printed back in the nineteen-*eighties*, for Goddess' sake! You're supposed to have the *new* edition, the one Anna Marie approved. This is *definitely* L1." Periwinkle throws the discredited volume over the side. "Bob Finch had a hand in all those old guides until '02. You can't trust anything from before then."

The wheelhouse hatch swings open. *Dipnet*'s captain, a gangly old salt whose ears look as though they've been attached upside-down, clears his throat. "Got a message coming in," he announces over the growl of the engine. "I'll put it on the speakers." The hatch swings shut.

A message! Of course, *Dipnet* has all the technology, the hydrophones, the computers, everything it needs for the unenlightened to communicate with both species. There's a speaker mounted on the roof of the cabin, pointing down at the rear deck. It burps static for a moment, then:

"Sisters. Hurry." A squeal of feedback. "Grandmother. Says. Hello."

Count on crass western technology to turn a beautiful alien tongue into pidgin English.

"Ooh," says someone at the gunwales. "Look." The orcas are pacing *Dipnet* on either side, rolling and breathing in perfect synch.

"They want us to follow them," Periwinkle says excitedly.

"Yes, they do," intones one of the telepaths. "I can *feel* it."

The orcas are so close to the boat they're almost touching the hull. *Dipnet* plows straight ahead. Just as well. The whales aren't leaving enough room for course changes anyway.

🐒

The chair on the gangway is obviously not meant for children. Ramona fusses with the straps, cranks the cross-hairs down to child-height. She offers patient instruction in the use of the harpoon. Papa-san hollers up instructions of his own in Japanese. Conflicting ones, apparently; Tetsuo, bouncing excitedly in the harness, gives nothing but grief. Herschel continues his cheerful instigation: *Hey, lady, we pay ten grand for this, we do it our way thank you so much.* He doesn't seem to have noticed that Ramona's smile shows more teeth than usual.

This looks very promising. Doug glances back over his shoulder; the route's still clear. *Fifty-five seconds ...*

Shamu rolls past on the other side of the plexi.

The crowd laughs. Doug turns back to center stage. Ramona's had enough; she's jumped down from Tetsuo's perch and is barking at Herschel in Japanese. Or maybe in sea lion. Herschel backs away, hands held up placatingly against Ramona's advance. It's entertaining enough, but Doug keeps his eyes on Tetsuo. The kid is the key. Adult squabbles don't interest a ten-year-old, he's strapped in at the controls of the best bloody video game since the parents' groups came down on Nintendo. If it's going to happen at all, Doug knows, it's going to happen—

Tetsuo squeezes the trigger.

—*Now.*

Ramona turns just in time to see the harpoon strike home. The crowd cheers. Tetsuo shrieks in delight. Shamu just shrieks, thrashing. A pink cloud puffs from his blowhole.

Doug is already half-turned, one foot raised to motor. He checks himself: *Wait for it, it still might be clean ...*

"*Shit!* You were supposed to *wait!*" Ramona's mike is off-line but it doesn't matter; you could hear that yell all the way over in the Arctic Exhibit. She brings her translator online, barks syllables. The ringside speakers chirp and whistle. Shamu whistles back, spasming as though electrocuted. His flukes churn the water into pink froth.

"His lung's punctured," Ramona calls over to the guy with the cattle prod. Prodmeister disappears backstage. Ramona wheels on Tetsuo. "You were supposed to wait until I told him to hold still! Do you *want* him to suffer? It'll take *days* to die from a hit like that!"

That's it. Go.

He knows what's coming. Herschel, out his ten thousand dollars, will demand that his son get another chance. The Aquarium will stand firm; ten grand buys one shot, not one kill. No, sir, you can't try again unless you're willing to pay.

Herschel's own shrieks will go ultrasonic. Prodmeister will come back with another harpoon, a bigger, no-nonsense harpoon this time. Perhaps the Guests will try and wrestle it away. *That's* resulted in an unfortunate accident or two.

Doesn't matter. Doug's not going to be around for any of it, he's already halfway out of the amphitheater. From the corner of his eye he can see his competition, caught flat-footed, just starting to rise from the bleachers. Some of them, closer to the main theater entrance, would still have a chance to beat him if he was going the usual route. He's not. Doug Largha may be the first person in recorded history to have actually *read* the award-winning educational displays in the underwater gallery, and that gives him all the edge he needs. That's where he's headed now, at top speed.

Herschel and his ten grand. Tetsuo and his lousy aim. Doug could kiss them both. When a guest makes a kill, they get to keep the carcass.

But when they fuck up, it's whale steaks in the gift shop.

Well, no one expected the whales to be such assholes.

Certainly not Anna Marie Hamilton and her army of whale-huggers. The Gospel according to Anna Marie said that orcas (you *never* called them "killer whales") were gentle, intelligent creatures who lived in harmonious matriarchal societies. Humans were ethically bound to respect their cultural autonomy. Kidnapping these creatures from the wild, tearing them from their nurturing female-centered family units and selling them into bondage for barbaric human entertainment — this went beyond mere animal abuse. This was slavery, pure and simple.

That was all before the Breakthrough, of course. These days, it's kind of hard to rail against the enslavement of orcas when every schoolkid knows that all orca society, Resident or Transient, is *based* on slavery. Always has been. The matriarchs aren't kindly nurturing feminist grandmas, they're eight-ton black-and-white Mommie Dearests with really big teeth. And their children aren't treasured guardians of the next generation, either. They're genetic commodities, a common currency for trade between pods, and who knew what uses they got put to? It's a scientific fact that almost half of all killer whales die before reaching their first birthday.

That infant-mortality stat has been a godsend to the aquarium industry ever since it was derived in the nineteen-seventies — *Well of course it's tragic that another calf died here in our habitat but you know, even in the wild killer whales just aren't very good parents* — but even the whalejailers were taken aback to be proven so utterly right. It didn't take them long to recover from the shock, though. To embrace the irrefutable evidence of this kindred intelligence. To see the error of their ways. To reach out across that immense interspecies gulf with a business proposition.

And what do you know. The Matriarchs were more than happy to cut a deal.

SLAVERS OF THE SEVEN SEAS, a wall-sized viewscreen shouts in capital letters. Beside it, smaller screens run looped footage already seen a million times in every living room on the continent: priests and politicians and longliners and whale-huggers, riding the *Friendship Flotilla* out into history to sign the first formal agreement with the Matriarch of J-Pod.

On the other side of the gallery, past two-inch plexi, the pinkness in the water is already starting to fade.

Doug skids to a halt in front of an orca family tree, no less boring for its catchy backlit-pastel-on-black color scheme. He scans the headings:

G12 Pod

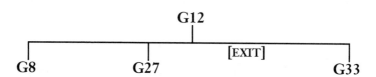

G12

G8   **G27**   [EXIT]   **G33**

There. Between G27 and G33. Evidently, municipal building codes require an emergency exit here. For some reason the aquarium has incorporated it into the Orca Family Tree, right there in plain sight as the law requires, but subtle, unobtrusive. In fact, damn near invisible to anyone who hasn't actually read the genealogies line-by-line.

This is Doug's secret passage. He's done his homework; the blueprints are on file at City Hall, accessible to anyone who cares to look. On the other side of this invisible door, backstage corridors run off in three separate directions, each servicing a different gallery. All of them, eventually, end up outside. One of them opens into the gift shop.

Doug pushes at a spot on the wall. It swings open. Behind him, a muffled *poomf* filters through from the main tank, followed by an inhuman squeal. Doug dives through the doorway without looking back.

Turn right. Run. Backstage, the gallery displays are ugly constructions of fiberglass and PVC. Every object gurgles or hums. Salt crusts everything. Doug's foot slips in a puddle. He starts to go over, grabs at the nearest handhold. A rack of hip waders topples in his stead. Left. Run. A row of filter pumps tears by on one side, a bank of holding tanks on the other. A dozen species of quarantined fish eye his transit with glassy indifference.

He rounds a corner. An unexpected barrier catches his shin. Doug sprawls across a stack of loose plywood. Splinters bury themselves in the balls of his hands.

"*Fuck!*" He scrambles to his feet, ignoring the pain. There are worse things than pain. There's the wrath of Alice if he comes home empty-handed.

Right there: a wood-paneled door. Not one of the crappy green metal doors that are good enough for the fishfeeders and janitors, but a nice oak job with a brass handle. That's got to be the entrance into the gift shop. He's almost there, and it's even *opening* for him, it's opening from the *other side* and he dives straight through, right into the waiting bosom of the woman coming from the other direction.

He thinks she looks familiar in the split second before they both go over. Doug catches a glimpse of someone else as a dozen vectors of force and inertia converge incompatibly on his ankle. There's a moment of brief, bright pain—

"*Owwwww!!!!!*"

—before he hits the floor. The good news is, he lands on a carpet with a very deep pile. The bad news is, rug burn tears most of the remaining skin off his palms.

He lies there, taking collect calls from every sensory nerve in his body. Two people are looking down at him. He forgets all about the pain when he recognizes who they are.

Saint Anna. And the Devil Himself.

Dipnet has arrived.

The perimeter is all around them: a float-line demarcated by warning buoys, a limited-entry circle a kilometer across. Scientists are only sometimes permitted here. Tourists are forbidden. But the gate swings open for *Dipnet*.

Now she chugs towards the center of the Communion Zone. The fog has partially lifted — the perimeter gate fades astern, while a tiny white dot resolves in the distance ahead. *Dipnet*'s escort remains close on either side. They've said nothing since that one brief message in the Strait, although the telepaths say the orcas are brimming with goodwill and harmony.

The floating dock is close enough to see clearly now, anchored in the center of the Zone, a white disk about twenty meters across. It seems featureless, beyond a few cleats for tying up. This is the way the orcas like things. This is *their* place, and they don't want it cluttered with nonessentials. A place to land, a space to stand, and Race Rocks looming out of the fog in the middle distance. Beyond that, only orcas and ocean.

"Is there a bathroom?" someone asks. The captain of the

Dipnet shakes his head, more in resignation than answer. He pulls back on the throttle while the mate, waiting on the fore-deck with a coil of nylon rope, jumps onto the platform and reels *Dipnet* in to dock.

"This is it, folks," the captain announces. "Everybody off."

The engine is still idling. "Aren't you going to tie up?" Periwinkle asks.

The captain shakes his head. "You're the ambassadors. We're just the taxi. They don't want us in the zone while you *commune*."

Periwinkle smiles patiently. She hears the resentment in the captain's voice, but she understands. It must be hard, seeing the Chosen Few going to make history while he just drives the boat. She feels sorry for him. She resolves to chant with him when he comes back to pick them up.

The captain grunts and waves her away. He sniffs and won-ders, not for the first time, if this woman remembered to clean the snails out of those shells before incorporating them into her own personal fashion statement. Or maybe it's one of those *nat-ural* fragrances they're advertising these days

The passengers file onto the platform. The first mate, still holding *Dipnet*'s leash, leaps back onto the foredeck. The boat growls backwards, changes gear, and wallows off into the haze. The sound of her engine fades with distance.

Eventually all is quiet again. The Chosen look about eagerly, not wanting to speak in this holy place. The orcas that guided them here have disappeared. Swells lap against the floats. The Race Rocks Lighthouse complains about the fog.

"Hey, you guys." It's the heretic again. He's watching the boat recede "When exactly are they supposed to be coming back for us?"

The others don't answer. This is a quiet moment, a *sacred* moment. It's no time to chatter about logistics. This guy doesn't know the first thing about reverence. Really, sometimes they wonder how he ever made the cut.

One whole Plexiglas wall looks into the turquoise arena of the killer whale tank; a pair of tail flukes disappear up through the

surface in ratcheting increments. The opposite wall serves as little more than a frame for the biggest flatscreen monitor Doug has ever seen. Murky green water swirls across that display. Wriggling wavelight reflects off a glass coffee table in the middle of the room. An antique oak desk looms behind it like a small wooden mesa.

In the middle of it all, Doug looks up from the floor at Anna Marie Hamilton and Bob Finch, executive director of the Aquarium. Anna Marie Hamilton and Bob Finch look back. This goes on for a moment or two.

"Can I help you, sir?" Finch asks at last.

"I — I think I got lost," Doug says, experimentally putting his foot down on the floor. It hurts, but it feels limpable, not broken.

"The viewing gallery is *that* way," Anna Marie announces, pointing to a different door than the one through which Doug arrived. "And I'm in the middle of some very tough negotiating, fighting for the freedom of our spiritual sib—"

"Actually, Ann — Ms. Hamilton, I suspect that Mr. — Mr. …"

"Largha," Doug says weakly.

"I suspect that Mr. Largha isn't all that interested in the boring details of our, er, negotiations." Finch extends a hand, helps Doug up off the carpet. Doug stands unsteadily.

"I was looking for — the *gift shop!*" His mission! Precious seconds, precious *minutes* irretrievably lost while all those other dorks and bozos line up to lay claim for *his* meat! If he doesn't come home with the steaks, he'll be sleeping on the sofa for a week. Doug turns and lunges towards the door he came through. He forgets all about his ankle for the half-second it takes for him to try and run on it. By the end of that same second he's on the floor again. "My steaks—" he whimpers. "I was going to be at the *head of the line* … I had it *planned to the second* …"

"Well, I must say," Finch extends a helping hand again, "it's heartening to see someone so enthusiastic about the Aquarium's new programs. Not everyone is, you know. Let me see what I can do."

Anna Marie Hamilton stands with her arms folded, sighing impatiently. "*Mister* Finch," she says, "if you think I'm going to let this *distract* me from the liberation of—"

"Not now, Ms. Hamilton. This will only take a moment. And then I promise, we can get right back to your tough and uncompromising negotiations." Finch takes a step towards the door, turns back to Doug. "Say, Mr. Largha, would you like to talk to a killer whale while you're waiting? A *Matriarch*? We have a live link to Juan de Fuca." He raises an arm to the flatscreen on one wall.

"Uh, live?" Emotions squabble in Doug's cortex. The pain of failure. The hope of salvation. And now, a vague discomfort. "I don't know. I mean, they *are* okay with this, aren't they? The whole whale show thing?"

"Mr. Largha, not only are they okay with it — it was their idea. So how about it? A conversation with a real, alien intelligence?"

"I don't know," Doug stammers. "I don't know what I'd *say*—"

Anna Marie snorts.

Finch draws a remote control from his blazer. "I'm sure you'll think of something." He points the remote at the flatscreen, thumbs a control.

Nothing obvious happens.

"Back in a moment," Finch promises, and closes the door behind him.

Anna Marie turns her back. Doug wonders if maybe she's offended by someone who would be in such a rush to line up for orca steaks.

Or maybe she just doesn't like people very much.

A long, mournful whistle. "Sister Predator," intones an artificial voice.

Doug turns to the flatscreen. A black-and-white shape looms up in the murky green wash of Juan de Fuca Strait. Lipless jaws open a crack; a zigzag crescent of conical teeth reflects gray in the dim light.

That whistle again. In one corner of the flatscreen, a flashing green tag: *Receiving*. "Fellow Sister Predator. Welcome."

Doug gawks.

Clicks. Two rapid-fire squeals. A moan. More clicks. *Receiving*.

"I am Second Grandmother. I trust you enjoy Aquarium and its many award-winning educational displays—"

Bzzt. In the upper left-hand corner of the screen: *Line Interrupt*. Silence.

At a panel on Finch's desk, Anna Marie Hamilton takes her finger off a red button.

"Wow," Doug says. "It was really talking."

Anna Marie rolls her eyes. "Yeah, well, it's not like they're going to beat us on the SAT's or anything."

A reporter waylays Bob Finch in a public corridor on his way to the gift shop. She seeks a reaction in the wake of Hamilton's demonstration. Finch considers. "We agree with the activists on one score. Orcas have their own values and their own society, and we're morally bound to respect their choices."

He smiles faintly. "Where Ms. Hamilton and I part ways, of course, is that she never bothered to find out what those values *were* before leaping to defend them."

The door opens. Finch the Savior stands in the doorway with a wooden box in one hand, a plastic bag in the other.

Doug, rising with his hopes off the couch, forgets all about the Matriarch and his ankle. "Are those my steaks?"

Finch smiles. "Mr. Largha, it takes several days to prepare the merchandise. Each sample has to be measured, weighed, and studied in accordance to our mandate of conservation through research."

"Oh, right." Doug nods. "I knew that."

"The gift shop is only taking a list of names."

"Right. "

"And unfortunately, all of today's specimen has already been spoken for. The line-up stretches all the way back into the Amazon gallery, in fact, so I brought a couple of items which I thought might do instead," Finch says. He holds up the bag. "There was quite a run on these, I was lucky to get one."

Doug squints at the label. "L'il Ahab Miniature Harpoon Kit. Rubber Tipped. Ages six and up."

"Everyone wants to prove that they're better shots than our

guests." Finch chuckles. "I suspect a lot of family dogs may be discomfited tonight. I thought your children might enjoy—"

"I don't have kids," Doug says. "But I have a dog." He takes the package. "What else?"

Finch holds out the wooden box. "I was able to locate some nice harbor seal—"

Finch the False Prophet. Finch the Betrayer.

"Harbor seal? *Harbor seal*! Your gift shop is *lousy* with harbor seal! It was marked *down*! My in-laws are coming over this weekend and you want me to feed them *harbor seal*? Why don't I just give them baloney sandwiches! My *dog* won't eat harbor seal!"

Finch shakes his head. He seems more saddened than offended. "I'm sorry you feel that way, Mr. Largha. I'm afraid there's nothing else we can do for you."

Doug wobbles dangerously on his good leg. "I was injured! In *your* aquarium! I'll sue!"

"If you *were* injured, Mr. Largha, you were injured en route from somewhere that you weren't legally supposed to be in the first place. Now, please ..." Finch opens the door a bit wider, just in case Doug hasn't got the point.

"Not supposed to *be* in! That was a fire exit route! Which, by the way," Doug's voice is becalmed by a sudden sense of impending victory, "was *improperly signed*."

Finch blinks. "Improperly—"

"You can barely *see* that exit sign," Doug says. "It's buried way down in one of those stupid orca family trees. If there was ever a fire, nobody would even *find* it. I mean, who stops to read *award-winning educational displays* when their pants are on fire?"

"Mr. Largha, the viewing gallery is solid cement on one side and a million gallons of seawater on the other. The odds of a fire are so minuscule—"

"We'll see whether the fire marshal's office thinks so. We'll see whether the *News at Six Consumer Advocate* thinks so!" Doug triumphantly folds his arms.

There is a moment of silence. Finally, Finch sighs and closes the door. "I'm really going to have to put my foot down with the art department about that. I mean, aesthetics or no aesthetics ..."

"I want my orca steaks," Doug says.

Finch walks to the wall behind his desk. A touch on a hidden control and a section of paneling slides away. Behind it, cigar boxes sit neatly arranged on grillwork shelves, lit by the unmistakable glow of a refrigerator lightbulb.

Finch turns around, one of the boxes open in his hands. Doug falls silent, disbelieving. It's not cigars in those boxes

"As I said, there are no orca steaks available," Finch begins. "But I *can* offer you some beluga sushi from my private stock."

Doug takes a hop forward. Another. It's almost *impossible* to get beluga. And this isn't the black-market, Saint-Lawrence beluga, the stuff that gives you mercury poisoning if you eat it more than twice a year. This is absolute primo *Hudson Bay* beluga. The only people harpooning *them* are a few captive Inuit on a natural habitat reserve out of Churchill, and even *they* only get away with it because they keep pushing the aboriginal rights angle. Nobody's figured out Belugan yet — from what Doug's heard, belugas are probably too stupid to even *have* a language — so nobody needs to cut a deal with them.

The box in Finch's hands costs about what Doug would make in a week.

"Will this be acceptable?" Bob Finch asks politely.

Doug tries to be cool. "Well, I suppose so."

He's almost sure they don't hear the squeak in his voice.

To the untrained eye, it looks like rambunctious play. In fact, the cavorting and splashing and bellyflopping is a synchronized and complex behavior. Co-operative hunting, it's called. First reported from the Antarctic, when a pod of killer whales was seen creating a mini-tidal wave to wash a crabeater seal off an ice floe. Definite sign of intelligence, that, the first mate's been told. He squints through his binoculars and the intermittent fog until the whales finish.

The first mate pulls open the wheelhouse hatch and climbs inside. The captain throws *Dipnet* into gear, singing:

And they'll know we are sisters by our love, by our—

The mate picks up the tune and rummages in a locker, surfaces with a bottle of Crown Royal. "Good show today." He raises the bottle in salute.

Doug Largha safely departed, Bob Finch extracts a pair of wineglasses from the shelves beneath the coffee table. He fills them from a convenient bottle of Chardonnay while Anna Marie taps a panel beside the flatscreen. The distant gurgling of Juan de Fuca fills the room once more.

Finch presents the activist with her glass. "Any problems on your end?"

Hamilton snorts, still fiddling one-handed with the controls. "You kidding? Turnover in the movement has always been high. And *nobody* turns down a chance to commune with the whales. It's a real adventure for them." The wall monitor flickers into splitscreen mode. One side still contains Juan de Fuca, newly restricted; the other shows one of the Aquarium's backstage holding tanks. A young male orca noses along its perimeter.

Finch raises his glass: first to the matriarch on the screen—"To your delicacies." Then to the matriarch in his office: "And to ours." Finally, he turns to the image of the holding tank. The whale there looks back at him with eyes like big black marbles.

"Welcome to the Aquarium," Finch says.

A signature whistle carries through the sound system. "Name is—" says the speaker. *No English Equivalent*, flashes the readout after a moment.

"That's a *fine* name," Finch remarks. "But why don't we give you a special new name? I think we'll call you — Shamu."

"Adventure," Shamu says. "Grandmother says this place adventure. Too small. I stay here long?"

Bob Finch glances at Anna Marie Hamilton.

Anna Marie Hamilton glances at Bob Finch.

"Not long, Grandson," says an alien voice from the cool distant waters of Juan de Fuca. "Not long at all."

Nimbus

She's been out there for hours now, listening to the clouds. I can see the Radio Shack receiver balanced on her knees, I can see the headphone wires snaking up and cutting her off from the world. Or connecting her, I suppose. Jess is hooked into the sky now, in a way I'll never be. She can hear it talking. The clouds advance, threatening grey anvils and mountains boiling in ominous slow motion, and the 'phones fill her head with alien grumbles and moans.

God she looks like her mother. I catch her profile and for a moment it *is* Anne there, gently chiding, *of course not, Jess, there aren't any spirits. They're just clouds.* But now I see her face and eight years have passed in a flash, and I know this can't be Anne. Anne knew how to smile.

I should go out and join her. It's still safe enough, we've got a good half hour before the storm hits. Not that it's really going to hit *us*; it's just passing through, they say, on its way to some other target. Still, I wonder if it knows we're in the way. I wonder if it cares.

I *will* join her. For once, I will not be a coward. My daughter sits five meters away in our own back yard, and I am damn well going to be there for her. It's the least I can do before I go.

I wonder if that will mean anything to her.

An aftermath, before the enlightenment.

It was as though somebody had turned the city upside down and shaken it. We waded through a shallow sea of detritus; broken walls, slabs of torn roofing, toilets and sofas and shattered glass. I walked behind Anne, Jess bouncing on my shoulders making happy gurgling noises; just over a year old, not quite talking yet but plenty old enough for continual astonishment. You could see it in her eyes. Every blown newspaper, every bird, every step was a new experience in wonder.

Also every loaded shotgun. Every trigger-happy national guardsman. This was a time when people still thought they owned things. They saw their homes strewn across two city blocks and the enemy they feared was not the weather, but each other. Hurricanes were accidents, freaks of nature. The experts were still blaming volcanoes and the greenhouse effect for everything. Looters, on the other hand, were real. They were tangible. They were a problem with an obvious solution.

The volunteers' shelter squatted in the distance like a circus tent at Armageddon. A tired-looking woman inside had given us shovels and pitchforks, and directed us to the nearest pile of unmanned debris. We began to pitch pieces of someone's life into an enormous blue dumpster. Anne and I worked side by side, stopping occasionally to pass Jessica back and forth.

I wondered what new treasures I was about to unearth. Some priceless family heirloom, miraculously spared? A complete collection of Jethro Tull CDs? Just a game, of course; the whole area had been combed, the owners had come and despaired of salvage, there was only wreckage beneath the wreckage. Still, every now and then I thought I saw something shining in the dirt, a bottle cap or a gum wrapper or a Rolex—

My pitchfork punched through a chunk of plaster and slid into something soft. It dropped suddenly under my weight, as if lubricated. It stopped.

I heard the muted hiss of escaping gas. Something smelled, very faintly, of rotten meat.

This isn't what I think it is. The crews have already been here. They used trained dogs and infrared scopes and they've already found all the bodies, they couldn't have missed anything there's nothing here but wood and plaster and cement—

I tightened my grip on the pitchfork, pulled up on the shaft. The tines rose up from the plaster, slick, dark, wet.

Anne was laughing. I couldn't believe it. I looked up, but she wasn't looking at me or the pitchfork or the coagulating stain. She was looking across the wreckage to a Ford pickup, loaded with locals and their rifles, inching its way down a pathway cleared in the road.

"Get a load of the bumper," she said, oblivious to my discovery.

There was a bumper sticker on the driver's side. I saw the caricature of a storm cloud, inside the classic red circle with diagonal slash. And a slogan.

A warning, to whom it may concern: *Clouds, we're gonna kick your ass.*

Jess takes off the headphones as I join her. She touches a button on the receiver. Cryptic wails, oddly familiar, rise from a speaker on the front of the device. We sit for a moment without speaking, letting the sounds wash over us.

Everything about her is so pale. I can barely see her eyebrows.

"Do they know where it's headed?" Jess asks at last.

I shake my head. "There's Hanford, but they've never gone after a reactor before. They say it might be trying to get up enough steam to go over the mountains. Maybe it's going after Vancouver or Sea-Tac again." I tap the box on her knees. "Hey, it might be laying plans even as we speak. You've been listening to that thing long enough, you should know what it's saying by now."

A distant flicker of sheet lightning strobes on the horizon. From Jessica's receiver, a dozen voices wail a discordant crescendo.

"Or you could even talk to it," I continue. "I saw the other day, they've got two-ways now. Like yours, only you can send as well as receive."

Jess fingers the volume control. "It's just a gimmick, Dad. These things couldn't put out enough power to get heard over all the other stuff in the air. TV, and radio, and …" She cocks her head at the sounds coming from the speaker. "Besides, nobody understands what they're saying anyway."

"Ah, but *they* could understand *us*," I say, trying for a touch of mock drama.

"Think so?" Her voice is expressionless, indifferent.

I push on anyway. Talking at least helps paper over my fear a bit. "Sure. The big ones could understand, anyway. A storm this size must have an IQ in the six digits, easy."

"I suppose," Jess says.

Inside, something tears a little. "Doesn't it *matter* to you?"

She just looks at me.

"Don't you want to know?" I say. "We're sitting here underneath this huge thing that nobody understands, we don't know what it's doing or why, and you sit there listening while it shouts at itself and you don't seem to care that it changed everything overnight—"

But of course, she doesn't remember that. Her memory doesn't go back to when we thought that clouds were just … clouds. She never knew what it was like to rule the world, and she never expects to.

My daughter is indifferent to defeat.

Suddenly, unbearably, I just want to hold her. *God Jess, I'm sorry we messed up so badly.* With effort, I control myself. "I just wish you could remember the way it was."

"Why?" she asks. "What was so different?"

I look at her, astonished. "Everything!"

"It doesn't sound like it. They say we *never* understood the weather. There were hurricanes and tornadoes even before, and sometimes they'd smash whole cities, and nobody could stop them then either. So what if it happens because the sky's alive, or just because it's, you know, random?"

Because your mother is dead, Jess, and after all these years I still don't know what killed her. Was it just blind chance? Was it the reflex of some slow, stupid animal that was only scratching an itch?

Can the sky commit murder?

"It matters," is all I tell her. Even if it doesn't make a difference.

The front is almost directly overhead now, like the mouth of a great black cave crawling across the heavens. West, all is clear. Above, the squall line tears the sky into jagged halves.

East, the world is a dark, murky green.

I feel so vulnerable out here. I glance back over my shoulder. The armoured house crouches at our backs, only the biggest trees left to keep it company. It's been eight years and the storms still haven't managed to dig us out. They got Mexico City, and Berlin, and the whole damn golden horseshoe, but our little house hangs in there like a festering cyst embedded in the landscape.

Then again, they probably just haven't noticed us yet.

Reprieved. The thing in the sky had gone to sleep, at least in our corner of the world. The source of its awareness — sources, rather, for they were legion — had convected into the stratosphere and frozen, a billion crystalline motes of suspended intellect. By the time they came back down they'd be on the other side of the world, and it would take days for the rest of the collective conscious to fill the gap.

We used the time to ready our defenses. I was inspecting the exoskeleton the contractors had just grafted onto the house. Anne was around front, checking the storm shutters. Our home had become monstrous, an angular fortress studded with steel beams and lightning rods. A few years earlier we would have sued anyone who did this to us. Today, we had gone into hock to pay for the retrofit.

I looked up at a faint roar from overhead. The sun reflected off a cluster of tiny cruciform shapes drawing contrails across the sky.

Cloud seeders. A common enough sight. In those days we still thought we could fight back.

"They won't work," Jess said seriously at my elbow.

I look down, startled. "Hey, Jess. Didn't see you sneaking up on me."

"They're just getting the clouds mad," she said, with all the certainty a four-year-old can muster. She squinted up into the blue expanse. "They're just trying to kill the, um, the messenger."

I squatted down, regarded her eye to eye. "And who told you that?" Not her mother, anyway.

"That woman. Talking to mom."

Not just a woman, I saw as I rounded the corner into the front yard. A couple: early twenties, mildly scruffy, both bearing slogans on their t-shirts. *Love Your Mother* the woman's chest told me, over a decal of the earth from lunar orbit. The man's shirt was more verbose: *Unlimited growth, the creed of carcinoma.* No room for a picture on that one.

Gaianists. Retreating across the lawn, facing Anne, as if afraid to turn their backs. Anne was smiling and waving, the very picture of inoffence, but I really felt for the poor bastards. They probably never knew what hit them.

Sometimes, when Seventh-Day Adventists came calling, Anne would actually invite them in for a little target practise. It was usually the Adventists who asked to leave.

"Did they have anything worthwhile to say?" I asked her now.

"Not really." Anne stopped waving and turned to face me. Her smile morphed into a triumphant smirk. "We're angering the sky gods, you know that? Thou shalt not inhabit a single-family dwelling. Thou shalt honour thy environmental impact, to keep it low."

"They could be right," I remarked. At least, there weren't many people around to argue the point. Most of our former neighbours had already retreated into hives. Not that *their* environmental impact had had much to do with it.

"Well, I'll grant it's not as flakey as some of the things they come up with," Anne admitted. "But if they're going to blame me for the revenge of the cloud demons, they damn well better have a rational argument or two waiting in the wings."

"I take it they didn't."

She snorted. "The same hokey metaphors. Gaia's leaping into action to fight the human disease. I guess hurricanes are supposed to be some sort of penicillin."

"No crazier than some of the things the experts say."

"Yeah, well, I don't necessarily believe them either."

"Maybe you should," I said. "I mean, *we* sure as hell don't know what's going on."

"And you think *they* do? Just a couple of years ago they were denying everything, remember? Life can't exist without stable organized structure, they said."

"I sort of thought they'd learned a few things since then."

"No kidding." Anne's eyes grew round with enlightenment. "And all this time I thought they were just making up trendy buzzwords."

Jess wandered between us. Anne scooped her up; Jess scrambled onto her mother's shoulders and surveyed the world from dizzying adult height.

I glanced back at the retreating evangelists. "So how did you handle those two?"

"I agreed with them," Anne said.

"Agreed?"

"Sure. We're a disease. Fine. Only some of us have mutated." She jerked a thumb at our castle. "Now, we're resistant to antibiotics."

We are resistant to antibiotics. We've encysted ourselves like hermit crabs. We've been pruned, cut back, decimated but not destroyed. We are only in remission.

But now, outside the battlements, we're naked. Even at this range the storm could reach out and swat us both in an instant. How can Jess just sit there?

"I can't even enjoy sunny days any more," I admit to her.

She looks at me, and I know her perplexity is not because I can't enjoy clear skies, but because I would even think it worthy of comment. I keep talking, refusing the chronic realization that we're aliens to each other. "The sky can be pure blue and sunshine, but if there's even one fluffy little cumulus bumping along I can't help feeling … watched. It doesn't matter if it's too small to think on its own, or that it'll dissipate before it gets a chance to upload. I keep thinking it's some sort of spy, it's going to report back somewhere."

"I don't think they can see," Jess says absently. "They just sense big things like cities and smokestacks, hot spots or things that … itch. That's all."

The wind breathes, deceptively gentle, in her hair. Above us a finger of grey vapour crawls between two towering masses of cumulo-nimbus. What's happening up there? A random conjunction of water droplets? A 25000-baud data dump between processing nodes? Even after all this time it sounds absurd.

So many eloquent theories, so many explanations for our downfall. Everyone's talking about order from chaos: fluid geometry, bioelectric microbes that live in the clouds, complex behaviours emerging from some insane alliance of mist and electrochemistry. It looks scientific enough on paper, but spoken aloud it always sounds like an incantation …

And none of it helps. The near distance is lit with intermittent flashes of light. The storm is walking toward us on jagged fractal legs. I feel like an insect under the heel of a descending boot. Maybe that's a positive sign. Would I be afraid if I had really given up?

Maybe. Maybe the situation is irrelevant. Maybe cowards are *always* afraid.

Jess's receiver is crying incessantly. "Whale songs," I hear myself say, and the tremor in my voice is barely discernible. "Humpback whales. That's what they sound like."

Jess fixes her eyes back on the sky. "They don't *sound* like anything, Dad. It's just electricity. Only the receiver sort of … makes it sound like something we know."

Another gimmick. We've fallen from God's chosen to endangered species in only a decade, and the hustlers still won't look up from their market profiles. I can sympathize. Looming above us, right now, are the ones who threw us into the street. The forward overhang is almost upon us. Ten kilometers overhead, winds are screaming past each other at sixty meters a second.

So far the storm isn't even breathing hard.

There was a banshee raging through the foothills. It writhed with tornados; Anne and I had watched the whirling black tentacles tearing at the horizon before we'd fled underground. Tornados were impossible during the winter, we'd been assured just a year before. Yet here we were, huddling together as the world shook, and all our reinforcements might as well have been made of paper if one of those figments came calling.

Sex is instinctive at times like those. Jeopardy reduces us to automata; there is no room for love when the genes reassert themselves. Even pleasure is irrelevant. We were just another pair of mammals, trying to maximize our fitness before the other shoe dropped.

Afterwards, at least, we were still allowed to feel. We clung together, blind and invisible in the darkness, almost crushing each other with the weight of our own desperation. We couldn't stop crying. I gave silent thanks that Jess had been trapped at daycare when the front came through. I wouldn't have stood the strain of a brave facade that night.

After a while, Anne stopped shaking. She lay in my arms, sniffling quietly. Dim floaters of virtual light swarmed maddeningly at the edge of my vison.

"The gods have come back," she said at last.

"Gods?" Anne was usually so bloody empirical.

"The old ones," she said. "The Old Testament gods. The Greek pantheon. Thunderbolts and fire and brimstone. We thought we'd outgrown them, you know? We thought …"

I felt a deep, trembling breath.

"*I* thought," she continued. "I thought we didn't need them any more. But we did. We fucked up so horribly on our own. There was nobody to keep us in line, and we trampled everything …"

I stroked her back. "Old news, Annie. You know we've cleaned things up. Hardly any cities allow gasoline any more, extinctions have levelled off. I even heard the other day that rainforest biomass increased last year."

"That's not *us*." A sigh whispered across my cheek. "We're no better than we ever were. We're just afraid of a spanking. Like spoiled kids caught drawing naughty pictures on the walls."

"Anne, we still don't know for sure if the clouds are really alive. Even if they are, that doesn't make them intelligent. Some people still say this is all just a weird side-effect of chemicals in the atmosphere."

"We're begging for mercy, Jon. That's all we're doing."

We breathed against dark, distant roaring for a few moments.

"At least we're doing something." I said at last. "Maybe we're not doing it for all the enlightened reasons we should be, but at least we're cleaning up. That's something."

"Not enough," she said. "We threw shit at something for centuries. How can a few prayers and sacrifices make it just go away and leave us alone? If it even exists. And if it *does* have any more brains than a flatworm. I guess you get the gods you deserve."

I tried to think of something to say, some twig of false reassurance. But, as usual, I wasn't fast enough. Anne picked herself up first:

"At least we've learned a little humility. And who knows?

Maybe the gods will answer our prayers before Jess grows up …"

They didn't. The experts tell us now that our supplications are on indefinite hold. We're praying to something that shrouds the whole planet, after all. It takes time for such a huge system to assimilate new information, more time to react. The clouds don't live by human clocks. We swarm like bacteria to them, doubling our numbers in an instant. How fast the response, from our microbial perspective? How long before the knee jerks? The experts mumble jargon among themselves and guess: decades. Maybe fifty years. This monster advancing on us now is answering a summons from the last century.

The sky screams down to fight with ghosts. It doesn't see me. If it sees anything at all, it is only the afterimage of some insulting sore, decades old, that needs to be disinfected. I lean against the wind. Murky chaos sweeps across something I used to call property. The house recedes behind me. I don't dare look but I know it must be kilometers away, and somehow I'm paralysed. This blind seething medusa claws its way towards me and its face covers the whole sky; how can I *not* look?

"*Jessica* …"

I can see her from the corner of my eye. With enormous effort, I move my head a little and she comes into focus. She is looking at the heavens, but her expression is not terrified or awed or even curious.

Slowly, smooth as an oiled machine, she lowers her eyes to earth and switches off the receiver. It hardly matters any more. The thunder is continuous, the wind is an incessant roar, the first hailstones are pelting down on us. If we stay out here we'll be dead in two hours. Doesn't she know it? Is this some sort of test, am I supposed to prove my love for her by facing down God like this?

Maybe it doesn't matter. Maybe now's the time. Maybe—

Jessica puts her hand on my knee. "Come on," she says, like a parent. "Let's go inside."

I am remembering the last time I saw Anne. I have no choice;

the moment traps me when I'm not looking, embeds me in a cross-section of time stopped dead when the lightning hit ten meters behind her:

The world is a flat mosaic in blinding black-and white, strobe-lit, motionless. Sheets of grey water are suspended in the act of slamming the earth. Anne is just out of reach, head down, her determination as clear as a kodalith snapshot in perfect focus: she is damn well going to make it to safety and she doesn't care what gets in her way. And then the lightning implodes into darkness, the world jerks back into motion with a sound like Hiroshima and the stench of burning electricity, but my eyes are shut tight, still fixed on that receding instant. There is sudden pain, small fingernails gouging the flesh of my palm, and I know that Jessica has not closed her eyes, that she knows more of this moment than I can bear to. I pray, for the only time in my life I pray to the sky *please let me be mistaken take someone else take me take the whole fucking city only please give her back I'm sorry I didn't believe ...*

Forty or fifty years from now, according to some, it might hear that. Too late for Anne. Too late even for me.

It's still out there. Just passing through, it drums its fingers on the ground and all our reinforced talismans can barely keep it out. Even here, in this underground sanctum, the walls are shaking.

It doesn't scare me any more.

There was another time, long ago, when I wasn't afraid. Back then the shapes in the sky were friendly; snow-covered mountains, magical kingdoms, once I even saw Anne up there. But now I only see something malign and hideous, ancient, something slow to anger and impossible to appease. In the thousands of years we spent watching the clouds, after all the visions and portents we read there, never once did we see the thing that was really looking back.

We see it now.

I wonder which epitaphs they'll be reading tomorrow. What city is about to be shattered by impossible tornados, how many will die in this fresh onslaught of hailstones and broken glass? I don't know. I don't even care. That surprises me. Just a few days ago, I think it would have mattered. Now, even the realization that we are spared barely moves me to indifference.

Jess, how can you sleep through this? The wind tries to uproot us, bits of God's brain bash themselves against our shelter, and somehow you can just curl up in the corner and block it out. You're so much older than I am, Jess; you learned not to care years ago. Barely any of you shines out any more. Even the glimpses I catch only seem like old photographs, vague reminders of what you used to be. Do I really love you as much as I tell myself?

Maybe all I love is my own nostalgia.

I gave you a start, at least. I gave you a few soft years before things fell apart. But then the world split in two, and the part I can live in keeps shrinking. You slip so easily between both worlds; your whole generation is amphibious. Not mine. There's nothing left I can offer you, you don't need me at all. Before long I'd have dragged you down with me.

I won't let that happen. You're half Anne, after all.

The maelstrom covers the sound of my final ascent. I wonder what Anne would think of me now. She'd disapprove, I guess. She was too much of a fighter to *ever* give up. I don't think she had a suicidal thought in her whole life.

And suddenly, climbing the stairs, I realize that I can ask her right now if I want to. Anne is watching me from a far dark corner of the room, through weathered adolescent eyes opened to mere slits. Is she going to call me back? Is she going to berate me for giving in, say that she loves me? I hesitate. I open my mouth.

But she closes her eyes without a word.

Flesh Made Word

Wescott was glad when it finally stopped breathing.

It had taken hours, this time. He had waited while it wheezed out thick putrid smells, chest heaving and gurgling and filling the room with stubborn reminders that it was only dying, not yet dead, not yet. He had been patient. After ten years, he had learned to be patient; and now, finally, the thing on the table was giving up.

Something moved behind him. He turned, irritated; the dying hear better than the living, a single spoken word could ruin hours of observation. But it was only Lynne, slipping quietly into the room. Wescott relaxed. Lynne knew the rules.

For a moment he even wondered why she was there.

Wescott turned back to the body. Its chest had stopped moving. *Sixty seconds*, he guessed. *Plus or minus ten.*

It was already dead by any practical definition. But there were still a few embers inside, a few sluggish nerves twitching in a brain choked with dead circuitry. Wescott's machines showed him the landscape of that dying mind: a topography of luminous filaments, eroding as he watched.

The cardiac thread shuddered and lay still.

Thirty seconds. Give or take five. The qualifiers came automatically. There is no truth. There are no facts. There is only the envelope of the confidence interval.

He could feel Lynne waiting invisibly behind him.

Wescott glanced at the table for a moment, looked away again; the lid over one sunken eye had crept open a crack. He could almost imagine he had seen nothing looking out.

Something changed on the monitors. *Here it comes …*

He didn't know why it scared him. They were only nerve impulses, after all; a fleeting ripple of electricity, barely detectable, passing from midbrain to cortex to oblivion. Just another bunch of doomed neurons, gasping.

And now there was only flesh, still warm. A dozen lines lay flat on the monitors. Wescott leaned over and checked the leads connecting meat to machine.

"Dead at nineteen forty-three," he said into his recorder. The machines, intelligent in their own way, began to shut themselves down. Wescott studied the dead face, peeled back the unclenched eyelid with a pair of forceps. The static pupil beneath stared past him, fixed at infinity.

You took the news well, Wescott thought.

He remembered Lynne. She was standing to one side, her face averted.

"I'm sorry," she said. "I know this is never a good time, but it's—"

He waited.

"It's Zombie," she went on. "There was an accident, Russ, he wandered out on the road and — and I took him into the vet's and she says he's too badly hurt but she won't put him to sleep without your consent, you never listed me as an owner—"

She stopped, like a flash flood ending.

He looked down at the floor. "Put him to sleep?"

"She said it's almost certain anything they tried wouldn't work, it would cost thousands and he'd probably die anyway—"

"You mean kill him. She won't kill him without my consent." Wescott began stripping the leads from the cadaver, lining them up on their brackets. They hung there like leeches, their suckers slimy with conductant.

"—and all I could think was, after eighteen years he shouldn't die alone, someone should be there with him, but I can't, you know, I just—"

Somewhere at the base of his skull, a tiny voice cried out *My Christ don't I go through enough of this shit without having to watch it happen to my own cat?* But it was very far away, and he could barely hear it.

He looked at the table. The corpse stared its cyclopean stare.

"Sure," Wescott said after a moment. "I'll take care of it." He allowed himself a half-smile. "All in a day's work."

The workstation sat in one corner of the living room, an ebony cube of tinted perspex, and for the past ten years it had spoken to him in Carol's voice. That had hurt at first, so much that he had nearly changed the program; but he had fought the urge, and beaten it, and endured the synthetic familiarity of her voice like a man doing penance for some great sin. Somewhere in the past decade the pain had faded below the level of conscious recognition. Now he heard it list the day's mail, and felt nothing.

"Jason Mosby called again from Southam," it said, catching Carol's intonation perfectly. "He s-still wants to interview you. He left a conversational program in my stack. You can run it any time you want."

"What else?"

"Zombie's collar stopped transmitting at nine sixteen, and Zombie didn't s-show up for his afternoon feed. Y-You might want to call around."

"Zombie's gone," he said.

"That's what I said."

"No, I mean—" *Christ, Carol. You never were much for euphemisms, were you?* "Zombie got hit by a car. He's dead."

Even when we tried using them on you.

"Oh. Shit." The computer paused a moment, some internal clock counting off a precise number of nanosecs. "I'm sorry, Russ."

It was a lie, of course, but a fairly convincing one all the same.

Outside, Wescott smiled faintly. "It happens. Just a matter of time for all of us."

There was a sound from behind. He turned away from the cube; Lynne stood in the doorway. He could see sympathy in her eyes, and something else.

"Russ," she said. "I'm so sorry."

He felt a twitch at the corner of his mouth. "So's the computer."

"How are you feeling?"

He shrugged. "Okay, I guess."

"I doubt it. You had him all those years."

"Yeah. I — miss him." There was a hard knot of vacuum in his throat. He examined the feeling, distantly amazed, and almost felt a kind of gratitude.

She padded across the room to him, took his hands. "I'm sorry I wasn't there at the end, Russ. It was all I could do to take him in. I just couldn't, you know—"

"It's okay," Wescott said.

"—and you had to be there anyway, you—"

"It's okay," he said again.

Lynne straightened and rubbed one hand across her cheek. "Would you rather not talk about it?" Which meant, of course, *I want to talk about it.*

He wondered what he could say that wouldn't be utterly predictable: and realised that he could afford to tell the truth.

"I was thinking," he said, "he had it coming to him."

Lynne blinked.

"I mean, he'd spread enough carnage on his own. Remember how every couple of days he'd bring in a wounded vole or a bird, and I never let him actually kill any of them—"

"You didn't want to see anything suffer," Lynne said.

"—so I'd kill them myself." One blow with a hammer, brains scrambled instantly, nothing left that *could* suffer after that. "I always spoiled his fun. It's such a drag having to play with dead things, he'd bitch at me for hours …"

She smiled sadly. "He was suffering, Russ. He wanted to die. I know you loved the little ingrate, we both did."

Something flared where the vacuum had been. "It's okay, Lynne. I watch *people* die all the time, remember? I'm in no great need of therapy over a fucking cat. And if I was, you could—"

—have at least been there this morning.

He caught himself. *I'm angry*, he realised. *Isn't that strange. I haven't used this feeling for years.*

It seemed odd that anything so old could have such sharp edges.

"Sorry," he said evenly. "I didn't mean to snap. It's just — I heard enough platitudes at the vet, you know? I'm sick of people saying *he wants to die* when they mean *It would cost too much*. And I'm especially sick of people saying *love* when they mean *economics.*"

Lynne put her arms around him. "There was nothing they could have done."

He stood there, swaying slightly, almost oblivious to her embrace.

Carol, how much did I pay to keep you breathing? And when did I decide you weren't worth the running tab?

"It's always economics," he said. And brought his arms up to hold her.

"You want to read minds."

Not Carol's voice, this time. This time it belonged to that guy from Southam ... Mosby, that was it. Mosby's program sat in memory, directing a chorus of electrons that came out sounding like he did, a cheap auditory clone. Wescott preferred it to the original.

"Read minds?" He considered. "Actually, right now I'm just trying to build a working model of one."

"Like me?"

"No. You're just a fancy menu. You ask questions; depending on how I answer them you branch to certain others. You're linear. Minds are more ... distributed."

"Thoughts are not signals, but the intersections of signals."

"You've read Penthorne."

"I'm reading him now. I've got Biomedical Abstracts online."

"Mmmm."

"I'm also reading Gödel," the program said. "If he's right, you'll never get an accurate model of the human brain, because no box is big enough to hold itself."

"So simplify it. Throw away the details, but preserve the essence. You don't want to make your model too big anyway; if it's as complicated as the real thing, it's just as hard to understand."

"So you just cut away at the brain until you end up with something simple enough to deal with?"

Wescott winced. "If you've got to keep it to vidbits, I guess that's as good as any."

"And what's left is still complex enough to teach you anything about human behaviour?"

"Look at you."

"Just a fancy menu."

"Exactly. But you know more than the real Jason Mosby. You're a better conversationalist, too; I met him once. I bet you'd even score higher on a Turing test. Am I right?"

A barely perceptible pause. "I don't know. Possibly."

"As far as I can tell you're better than the original, and with only a few percent of the processing power."

"Getting back to—"

"And if the original screams and fights when somebody tries to turn him off," Wescott went on, "It's just because he's been programmed to think he can suffer. He puts a bit more effort into keeping his subroutines running. Maybe not much of a difference after all, hmmm?"

The program fell silent. Wescott started counting: *one one thousand, two one thousand, three—*

"That actually brings up another subject I wanted to ask you about," the menu said.

Almost four seconds to respond, and even then it had had to change the subject. It had limits. Good program, though.

"You haven't published anything on your work at VanGen," Mosby's proxy remarked. "I'm unable to access your NSERC proposal, of course, but judging from the public abstract you've been working on dead people."

"Not dead. Dying."

"Near-death experiences? Levitation, tunnel of light, that sort of thing?"

"Symptoms of anoxia," Wescott said. "Mostly meaningless. We go further."

"Why?"

"A few basic patterns are easier to record after other brain functions have shut down."

"What patterns? What do they tell you?"

They tell me there's only one way to die, Mosby. It doesn't matter what kills you, age or violence or disease, we all sing out the same damn song before we cash in. You don't even have to be human; as long as you've got a neocortex you're part of the club.

And you know what else, Mosby? We can almost read the lyric sheet.

Come by in person, say a month from now, and I could preview your own last thoughts for you. I could give you the scoop of the decade.

"Dr. Wescott?"

He blinked. "Sorry?"

"What patterns? What do they tell you?"

"What do you think?" Wescott said, and started counting again.

"I think you watch people die," the program answered, "and you take pictures. I don't know why. But I think our subscribers would like to."

Wescott was silent for a few moments.

"What's your release number?" he asked at last.

"Six point five."

"You're just out, aren't you?"

"April fifteenth," the program told him.

"You're better than six four."

"We're improving all the time."

From behind, the sound of an opening door. "Stop," Wescott said.

"Do you want to c-cancel the program or just suspend it?" Carol's voice asked from the cube.

"Suspend." Wescott stared at the computer, vaguely jarred by the change in voice. *Do they ever feel crowded in there?*

"Can you hear it?" Lynne said from behind him.

He turned in his chair. She was taking off her shoes by the front door.

"Hear what?" Wescott asked.

She came across the room. "The way her voice sort of — catches, sometimes?"

He frowned.

"Like she was in pain when she made the recording," she went on. "Maybe it was before she was even diagnosed. But when she programmed that machine, it picked up on it. You've never heard it? In all these years?"

Wescott said nothing.

Lynne put her hands on his shoulders. "You sure it isn't time to change the personality in that thing?" she asked gently.

"It's not a personality, Lynne."

"I know. Just a pattern-matching algorithm. You keep saying that."

"Look, I don't know what you're so worried about. It's no threat to you."

"I didn't mean—"

"Eleven years ago she talked to it for a while. It uses her speech patterns. It isn't her. I know that. It's just an old operating system that's been obsolete for the better part of a decade."

"Russ—"

"That lousy program Mosby sent me is ten times more sophisticated. And you can go out and buy a psyche simulator that will put *that* to shame. But this is all I have left, okay? The least you can do is grant me the freedom to remember her the way I choose."

She pulled back. "Russ, I'm not trying to fight with you."

"I'm glad." He turned back to the workstation. "Resume."

"Suspend," Lynne said. The computer waited silently.

Wescott took a slow breath and turned back to face her.

"I'm not one of your patients, Lynne." His words were measured, inflectionless. "If you can't leave your work downtown, at least find someone else to practise on."

"Russ …" Her voice trailed off.

He looked back at her, utterly neutral.

"Okay, Russ. See you later." She turned and walked back to the door. Wescott noted the controlled tetanus in her movements, imagined the ratchet contraction of actomyosin as she reached for her shoes.

She's running, he thought, fascinated. *My words did that to her. I make waves in the air and a million nerves light up her brain like sheet lightning. How many ops/sec happening in there? How many switches opening, closing, rerouting, until some of that electricity runs down her arm and makes her hand turn the doorknob?*

He watched her intricate machinery close the door behind itself.

She's gone, he thought. *I've won again.*

Wescott watched Hamilton strap the chimp onto the table

and attach the leads to its scalp. The chimp was used to the procedure; it had been subject to such indignities on previous occasions, and had always survived in good health and good spirits. There was no reason for it to expect anything different this time.

As Hamilton snugged the straps, the smaller primate stiffened and hissed.

Wescott studied a nearby monitor. "Damn, it's nervous." Cortical tracings, normally languorous, scrambled across the screen in epileptic spasms. "We can't start until it calms down. *Unless* it calms down. Shit. This could scotch the whole recording."

Hamilton pulled one of the restraints a notch tighter. The chimp, its back pulled flat against the table, flexed once and went suddenly limp.

Wescott looked back at the screen. "Okay, it's relaxing. Showtime, Pete; you're on in about thirty seconds."

Hamilton held up the hypo. "Ready."

"Okay, getting baseline — now. Fire when ready."

Needle slid into flesh. Wescott reflected on the obvious unhumanity of the thing on the table; too small and hairy, all bow legs and elongate simian arms. *A machine. That's all it is. Potassium ions jumping around in a very compact telephone switchboard.*

But the eyes, when he slipped and looked at them, looked back.

"Midbrain signature in fifty seconds," Wescott read off. "Give or take ten."

"Okay," Hamilton said. "It's going through the tunnel."

Just a machine, running out of fuel. A few nerves sputter and the system thinks it sees lights, feels motion—

"There. Thalamus," Hamilton reported. "Right on time. Now it's in the ret." A pause. "Neocortex, now. Same damn thing every time."

Wescott didn't look. He knew the pattern. He had seen its handwriting in the brains of a half a dozen species, watched that same familiar cipher scurry through dying minds in hospital beds and operating theatres and the twisted wreckage of convenient automobiles. By now he didn't even need the machines to see it. He only had to look at the eyes.

Once, in a moment of reckless undiscipline, he'd wondered if he were witnessing the flight of the soul, come crawling to the surface of the mind like an earthworm flushed by heavy rains. Another time he'd thought he might have captured the EEG of the Grim Reaper.

He no longer allowed himself such unbridled licence. Now he only stared at the widening pupils within those eyes, and heard the final panicked bleating of the cardiac monitor.

Something behind the eyes went out.

What were you? he wondered.

"Dunno yet," Hamilton said beside him. "But another week, two at the outside, and we've got it nailed."

Wescott blinked.

Hamilton started unstrapping the carcass. After a moment he looked up. "Russ?"

"It knew." Wescott stared at the monitor, all flat lines and static now.

"Yeah." Hamilton shrugged. "I wish I knew what tips them off sometimes. Save a lot of time." He dumped the chimp's body into a plastic bag. Its dilated pupils stared out at Wescott in a grotesque parody of human astonishment.

"—Russ? You okay?"

He blinked; the dead eyes lost control. Wescott looked up and saw Hamilton watching him with a strange expression.

"Sure," he said easily. "Never better."

There was this cage. Something moved inside that he almost recognised, a small furred body that looked familiar. But up close he could see his mistake. It was only a wax dummy, or maybe an embalmed specimen the undergrads hadn't got to yet. There were tubes running into it at odd places, carrying sluggish aliquots of yellow fluid. The specimen jaundiced, bloated as he watched. He reached through the bars of the cage ... he could do that somehow, even though the gaps were only a few centimeters wide ... and touched the thing inside. Its eyes opened and stared past him, blank and blind with pain; and their pupils were not vertical as he had expected, but round and utterly human ...

He felt her awaken in the night beside him, and not move.

He didn't have to look. He heard the change in her breathing, could almost feel her systems firing up, her eyes locking onto him in the near-darkness. He lay on his back, looking up at a ceiling full of shadow, and did not acknowledge her.

He turned his face to stare at the faint grey light leaking through the window. Straining, he could just hear distant city sounds.

He wondered, for a moment, if she hurt as much as he did; then realised that there was no contest. The strongest pain he could summon was mere aftertaste.

"I called the vet today," he said. "She said they didn't need my consent. They didn't need me there at all. They would have shut Zombie down the moment you brought him in, only you told them not to."

Still she did not move.

"So you lied. You fixed it so I'd have to be there, watching one more piece of my life getting—" he took a breath, "—chipped away—"

At last she spoke: "Russ—"

"But you don't hate me. So why would you put me through that? You must have thought it would be good for me, some-how."

"Russ, I'm sorry. I didn't mean to hurt you."

"I don't think that's entirely true," he remarked.

"No. I guess not." Then, almost hopefully, "It did hurt, didn't it?"

He blinked against a brief stinging in his eyes. "What do you think?"

"I think, nine years ago I moved in with the most caring, humane person I'd ever known. And two days ago I didn't know if he'd give a damn about the death of a pet he'd had for eight-een years. I really didn't know, Russ, and I'm sorry but I had to find out. Does that make sense?"

He tried to remember. "I think you were wrong from the start. I think you gave me too much credit nine years ago."

He felt her head shake. "Russ, after Carol died I was afraid *you* were going to. I remember hoping I'd never be able to hurt that much over another human being. I fell in love with you because you could."

"Oh, I loved her all right. A hundred grand's worth at least. Never did get around to figuring out her final worth."

"That's not why you did it! You remember how she was suffering!"

"Actually, no. She had all those — painkillers, cruising through her system. That's what they told me. By the time they started cutting pieces out of her she was — numb ..."

"Russ, I was there too. They said there was no hope, she was in constant pain, they said she'd want to die—"

"Oh yes. Later, that's what they said. When it was time to decide. Because they knew ..."

He stopped.

"They knew," he said again, "what I wanted to hear."

Beside him, Lynne grew very still.

He laughed once, softly. "I shouldn't have been so easy to convince, though. I knew better. We're not hardwired for Death with Dignity; life's been kicking and clawing and doing anything it can to take a few more breaths, for over three billion years. You can't just decide to turn yourself off."

She slid an arm across his chest. "People turn themselves off all the time, Russ. Too often. You know that."

He didn't answer. A distant siren poisoned the emptiness.

"Not Carol," he said after a while. "I sort of made that decision for her."

Lynne put her head on his shoulder. "And you've spent ten years trying to find out if you guessed right. But they're not *her*, Russ, all the people you've recorded, all the animals you've ... put down, they're not *her*—"

"No. They're not." He closed his eyes. "They don't linger on month after month. They don't ... shrivel up ... you *know* they're going to die, and it's always quick, you don't have to come in day after day, watching them change into something that, that *rattles* every time it breathes, that doesn't even know who you are and you wish it would just—"

Wescott opened his eyes.

"I keep forgetting what you do for a living," he said.

"Russ—"

He looked over at her, calmly. "Why are you doing this to me?

You think I haven't already been over it enough?"

"Russ, I'm only—"

"Because it won't work, you know. It's too late. It took long enough, but I know how the mind works now, and you know what? It's nothing special after all. It's not spiritual, it's not even quantum. It's just a bunch of switches wired together. So it doesn't matter if people can't speak their minds. Pretty soon I'll be able to *read* them."

His voice was level and reasoned. He kept his eyes on the ceiling; the darkened light fixture there seemed to waver before his eyes. He blinked, and the room swam suddenly out of focus.

She reached up to touch the wetness on his face. "It scares you," she whispered. "You've been chasing it for ten years and you've almost got it and it scares the shit out of you."

He smiled and wouldn't look at her. "No. That isn't it at all."

"What, then?"

He took a breath. "I just realised. I don't care one way or the other any more."

He came home, clutching the printout, and knew from the sudden emptiness of the apartment that he had been defeated here as well.

The workstation slept in its corner. Several fitful readouts twinkled on one of its faces, a sparse autonomic mosaic. He walked towards it; and halfway there one face of the cube flashed to life.

Lynne, from the shoulders up, looked out at him from the screen.

Wescott glanced around the room. He almost called out.

On the cube, Lynne's lips moved. "Hello, Russ," they said.

He managed a short laugh. "Never thought I'd see you in there."

"I finally tried one of these things. You were right, they've come a long way in ten years."

"You're a real simulation? Not just a fancy conversational routine?"

"Uh huh. It's pretty amazing. It ate all sorts of video footage, and all my medical and academic records, and then I had to talk with it until it got a feel for who I was."

And who is that? he wondered absently.

"It changed right there while I was talking to it, Russ. It was really spooky. It started out in this dead monotone, and as we talked it started mimicking my voice, and my mannerisms, and in a little while it sounded just like me, and here it is. It went from machine to human in about four hours."

He smiled, not easily, because he knew what was coming next.

"It — actually, it was a bit like watching a time-lapse video of you over the past few years," the model said. "Played backwards."

He kept his voice exactly level. "You're not coming home."

"Sure I am, Russ. Only home isn't here any more. I wish it were, you don't know how badly I wish it were, but you just can't let it go and I can't live with that any more."

"You still don't understand. It's just a program that happens to sound like Carol did. It's nothing. I'll — wipe it if it's that important to you—"

"That's not all I'm talking about, Russ."

He thought of asking for details, and didn't.

"Lynne—" he began.

Her mouth widened. It wasn't a smile. "Don't ask, Russ. I can't come back until you do."

"But I'm right here!"

She shook her head. "The last time I saw Russ Wescott, he cried. Just a little. And I think — I think he's been hunting something for ten years, and he finally caught a glimpse of it and it was too big, so he went away and left some sort of autopilot in charge. And I don't blame him, and you're a very good likeness, really you are but there's nothing in you that knows how to feel."

Wescott thought of acetycholinesterase and endogenous opioids. "You're wrong, Carol. I know more about feelings than almost anyone in the world."

On the screen, Lynne's proxy sighed through a faint smile.

The simulation was wearing new earrings; they looked like antique printed circuits. Wescott wanted to comment on them, to compliment or criticise or do anything to force the conversation into less dangerous territory. But he was afraid that she had worn them for years and he just hadn't noticed, so he said nothing.

"Why couldn't you tell me yourself?" he said at last. "Don't I deserve that much? Why couldn't you at least leave me in person?"

"This *is* in person, Russ. It's as in person as you ever let anyone get with you any more."

"That's bullshit! Did I *ask* you to go out and get yourself simmed? You think I see you as some sort of cartoon? My Christ, Lynne—"

"I don't take it personally, Russ. We're all cartoons as far as you're concerned."

"What in Christ's name are you talking about?"

"I don't blame you, really. Why learn 3-d chess when you can reduce it down to tic-tac-toe? You understand it perfectly, and you always win. Except it isn't that much fun to play, of course …"

"Lynne—"

"Your models only simplify reality, Russ. They don't recreate it."

Wescott remembered the printout in his hand. "Sure they do. Enough of it, anyway."

"So." The image looked down for a moment. *Uncanny, the way it fakes and breaks eye contact like that*— "You have your answer."

"*We* have the answer. Me, and a few terabytes of software, and a bunch of colleagues, Lynne. People. Who work with me, face to face."

She looked up again, and Wescott was amazed that the program had even mimicked the sudden sad brightness her eyes would have had in that moment. "So what's the answer? What's at the end of the tunnel?"

He shrugged. "Not much, after all. An anticlimax."

"I hope it was more than that, Russ. It killed us."

"Or it could've just been an artefact of the procedure. The old observer effect, maybe. Common sense could have told us as much, I could've saved myself the—"

"Russ."

He didn't look at the screen.

"There's nothing down there at all," he said, finally. "Nothing that thinks. I never liked it down there, it's all just … raw instinct, at the center. Left over from way back when the limbic system *was* the brain. Only now it's just unskilled labour, right? Just one small part of the whole, to do all that petty autonomic shit the upstart neocortex can't be bothered with. I never even considered that it might still be somehow … alive …"

His voice trailed off. Lynne's ghost waited silently, perhaps unequipped to respond. Perhaps programmed not to.

"You die from the outside in, did you know that?" he said, when the silence hurt more than the words. "And then, just for a moment, the center is all you are again. And down there, nobody wants to … you know, even the suicides, they were just fooling themselves. Intellectual games. We're so fucking proud of thinking ourselves to death that we've forgotten all about the old reptilian part sleeping inside, the part that doesn't calculate ethics or quality of life or burdens on the next of kin, it just wants to *live*, that's all it's programmed for, you know? And at the very end, when we aren't around to keep it in line any more, it comes up and looks around and at that last moment it knows it's been betrayed, and it … screams …"

He thought he heard someone speak his name, but he didn't look up to find out.

"That's what we always found," he said. "Something waking up after a hundred million years, scared to death …"

His words hung there in front of him.

"You don't know that." Her voice was distant, barely familiar, with a sudden urgency to it. "You said yourself it could be an artefact. She might not have felt that way at all, Russ. You don't have the data."

"Doesn't matter," he murmured. "Wetware always dies the same way—"

He looked up at the screen.

And the image was for Chrissakes *crying*, phosphorescent tears on artificial cheeks in some obscene parody of what Lynne would do if she had been there. Wescott felt sudden hatred for the software that wept for him, for the intimacy of its machine intuition, for the precision of its forgery. For the simple fact that it *knew* her.

"No big deal," he said. "Like I said, an anticlimax. Anyhow, I suppose you have to go back and report to your — body—"

"I can stay if you want. I know how hard this must be for you, Russ—"

"No you don't." Wescott smiled. "Lynne might have. You're

just accessing a psych database somewhere. Good try, though."

"I don't have to go, Russ—"

"Hey, that's not who I am any more. Remember?"

"—we can keep talking if you want."

"Right. A dialogue between a caricature and an autopilot."

"I don't have to leave right away."

"Your algorithms's showing," he said, still smiling. And then, tersely: "Stop."

The cube darkened.

"Do y-ou want to cancel the program or just suspend it?" Carol asked.

He stood there for a while without answering, staring into that black featureless cube of perspex. He could see nothing inside but his own reflection.

"Cancel," he said at last. "And delete."

Ambassador

First Contact was supposed to solve everything.

That was the rumour, anyway: gentle wizards from Epsilon Eridani were going to save us from the fire and welcome us into a vast Galactic Siblinghood spanning the Milky Way. Whatever diseases we'd failed to conquer, they would cure. Whatever political squabbles we hadn't outgrown, they would resolve. They were going to fix it all.

They were not supposed to turn me into a hunted animal.

I didn't dwell much on the philosophical implications, at first; I was too busy running for my life. *Zombie* streaked headlong into the universe, slaved to a gibbering onboard infested with static. Navigation was a joke. Every blind jump I made reduced the chances of finding my way home by another order of magnitude. I did it anyway, and repeatedly; any jump I *didn't* make would kill me.

Once more out of the breach. Long-range put me somewhere in the cometary halo of a modest binary. In better times the computer would have shown me the system's planetary retinue in an instant; now it would take days to make the necessary measurements.

Not enough time. I could have fixed my position in a day or so using raw starlight even without the onboard, but whatever was after me had never given me the chance. Several times I'd made a start. The longest reprieve had lasted six hours; in that time I'd placed myself somewhere coreward of the Orion spur.

I'd stopped trying. Knowing my location at any moment would put me no further ahead at t+1. I'd be lost again as soon as I jumped.

And I always jumped. It always found me. I still don't know

how; theoretically it's impossible to track anything through a singularity. But somehow space always opened its mouth and the monster dropped down on me, hungry and mysterious. It might have been easier to deal with if I'd known why.

What did I do, you ask. What did I do to get it so angry? Why, I tried to say hello.

What kind of intelligence could take offence at *that*?

Imagine a dead tree, three hundred fifty meters tall, with six gnarled branches worming their way from its trunk. Throw it into orbit around a guttering red dwarf that doesn't even rate a proper name. This is what I'd come upon; there were no ports, no running lights, no symbols on the hull. It hung there like some forgotten chunk of cosmic driftwood. Embers of reflected sunlight glinted occasionally from the surface; they only emphasised the shadows drowning the rest of the structure. I thought it was derelict at first.

Of course I went through the motions anyway. I reached out on all the best wavelengths, tried to make contact a hundred different ways. For hours it ignored me. Then it sent the merest blip along the hydrogen band. I fed it into the onboard.

What else do you do with an alien broadcast?

The onboard had managed one startled hiccough before it crashed. All the stats on my panel had blinked once, in impossible unison, and gone dark.

And then doppler had registered the first incoming missile.

So I'd jumped, blind. There really hadn't been a choice, then or the four times since. Sometime during that panicked flight, I had given my tormentor a name: *Kali*.

Unless *Kali* had gotten bored — hope springs eternal, even within puppets such as myself — I'd have to run again in a few hours. In the meantime I aimed *Zombie* at the binary and put her under thrust. Open space is impossible to hide in; a system, even a potential one, is marginally better.

Of course I'd have to jump long before I got there. It didn't matter. My reflexes were engineered to perform under all circumstances. *Zombie's* autopilot may have been disabled, but mine engaged smoothly.

It takes time to recharge between jumps. So far, it had taken longer for *Kali* to find me. At some point that was likely to change; the onboard had to be running again before it did.

I knew there wasn't a hope in hell.

A little forensic hindsight, here: how exactly did *Kali* pull it off?

I'm not exactly sure. But some of *Zombie*'s diagnostic systems run at the scale of the merely electronic, with no reliance on quantum computation. The crash didn't affect them; they were able to paint a few broad strokes in the aftermath.

The Trojan signal contained at least one set of spatial co-ordinates. The onboard would have read that as a pointer of some kind: it would have opened the navigation files to see what resided at x-y-z. A conspicuous astronomical feature, perhaps? Some common ground to compare respective visions of time and space?

Zap. Nav files gone.

Once nav was down — or maybe before, I can't tell — the invading program told *Zombie* to update all her backups with copies of itself. Only then, with all avenues of recovery contaminated, had it crashed the onboard. Now the whole system was frozen, every probability wave collapsed, every qubit locked into P=1.00.

It was an astonishingly beautiful assault. In the time it had taken me to say hello, *Kali* had grown so intimate with my ship that she'd been able to seduce it into suicide. Such a feat was beyond my capabilities, far beyond those of the haphazard beasts that built me. I'd have given anything to meet the mind behind the act, if it hadn't been trying so hard to kill me.

Early in the hunt I'd tried jumping several times in rapid succession, without giving *Kali* the chance to catch up. I'd nearly bled out the reserves. All for nothing; the alien found me just as quickly, and I'd had barely enough power to escape.

I was still paying for that gamble. It would take two days at sublight for *Zombie* to recharge fully, and ninety minutes before I could even jump again. Now I didn't dare jump until the destroyer came for me; I lay in real space and hoarded whatever moments of peace the universe saw fit to grant.

This time the universe granted three and a half hours. Then short-range beeped at me; object ahead. I plugged into *Zombie's* cameras and looked forward.

A patch of stars disappeared before my eyes.

The manual controls were still unfamiliar. It took precious seconds to call up the right numbers. Whatever eclipsed the stars was preceding *Zombie* on a sunwards course, decelerating fast. One figure refused to settle; the mass of the object was increasing as I watched. Which meant that it was coming through from somewhere else.

Kali was cutting her search time with each iteration.

Two thousand kilometres ahead, twisted branches turned to face me across the ether. One of them sprouted an incandescent bud.

Zombie's sensors reported the incoming missile to the onboard; the brainchips behind my dash asked for an impact projection. The onboard chittered mindlessly.

I stared at the approaching thunderbolt. *What do you want with me? Why can't you just leave me alone?*

Of course I didn't wait for an answer. I jumped.

My creators left me a tool for this sort of situation: *fear*, they called it.

They didn't leave much else. None of the parasitic nucleotides that gather like dust whenever blind stupid evolution has its way, for example. None of the genes that build genitals; what would have been the point? They left me a sex drive, but they tweaked it; the things that get me off are more tightly linked to mission profiles than to anything so vulgar as procreation. I retain a smattering of chemical sexuality, mostly androgens so I won't easily take no for an answer.

There are genetic sequences, long and intricately folded, which code for loneliness. Thigmotactic hardwiring, tactile pleasure, pheromonal receptors that draw the individual into social groups. All gone from me. They even tried to cut religion out of the mix, but God, it turns out, is borne of fear. The loci are easy enough to pinpoint but the linkages are absolute: you can't exorcise faith without eliminating pure mammalian terror as well. And out here, they decided, fear was too vital a survival mechanism to leave behind.

So fear is what they left me with. Fear, and superstition. And try as I might to keep my midbrain under control, the circuitry down there kept urging me to grovel and abase itself before the omnipotence of the Great Killer God.

I almost envied *Zombie* as she dropped me into another impermanent refuge. *Zombie* moved on reflex alone, braindead, galvanic. She didn't know enough to be terrified.

For that matter, I didn't know much more.

What was *Kali*'s problem, anyway? Was its captain insane, or merely misunderstood? Was I being hunted by something innately evil, or just the product of an unhappy childhood?

Any intelligence capable of advanced spaceflight must also be able to understand peaceful motives; such was the wisdom of Human sociologists. Most had never left the solar system. None had actually encountered an alien. No matter. The logic seemed sound enough; any species incapable of controlling their aggression probably wouldn't survive long enough to escape their own system. The things that made me nearly didn't.

Indiscriminate hostility against anything that moves is not an evolutionary strategy that makes sense.

Maybe I'd violated some cultural taboo. Perhaps an alien captain had gone insane. Or perhaps I'd chanced upon a battleship engaged in some ongoing war, wary of doomsday weapons in sheep's clothing.

But what were the odds, really? In all the universe, what are the chances that our first encounter with another intelligence would happen to involve an alien lunatic? How many interstellar wars would have to be going on simultaneously before I ran significant odds of blundering into one at random?

It almost made more *sense* to believe in God.

I searched for another answer that fitted. I was still looking two hours later, when *Kali* bounced my signal from only a thousand kilometres off.

Somewhere else in space, the question and I appeared at the same time: *is* everyone *out here like this*?

Assuming that I wasn't dealing with a statistical fluke — that I hadn't just happened to encounter one psychotic alien amongst a trillion sane ones, and that I hadn't blundered into the midst of some unlikely galactic war — there was one other alternative.

Kali was typical.

I put the thought aside long enough to check the Systems monitor; nearly two hours, this time, before I could jump again. *Zombie* was deeply interstellar, over six lightyears from the nearest system. Even I couldn't justify kicking in the thrusters at that range. Nothing to do but wait, and wonder—

Kali *couldn't* be typical. It made no sense. Maybe this was all just some fantastic cross-cultural miscommunication. Maybe *Kali* had mistaken my own transmission as some kind of attack, and responded in kind.

Right. An intelligence smart enough to rape my onboard in a matter of hours, yet too stupid to grasp signals expressly designed to be decipherable by *anyone*. *Kali* hadn't needed prime number sequences or pictograms to understand me or my overtures. It knew *Zombie's* mind from the qubits up. It knew that I was friendly, too. It had to know.

It just didn't care.

And barely ten minutes past the jump threshold, it finally caught up with me.

I could feel space rippling almost before the short-range board lit up. My inner ears split into a dozen fragments, each insisting *up* was a different direction. At first I thought *Zombie* was jumping by herself; then I thought the onboard gravity was failing somehow.

Then *Kali* began materialising less than a hundred meters away. I was caught in her wake.

I moved without thinking. *Zombie* spun on her axis and leapt away under full thrust. Telltales sparkled in crimson protest. Behind me, the plasma cone of *Zombie's* exhaust splashed harmlessly against the resolving monster.

Still wanting for solid substance, *Kali* turned to follow. Her malformed arms, solidifying, reached out for me.

It's going to grapple, I realised. Something subcortical screamed *Jump!*

Too close. I'd drag *Kali* through with me if I tried.

Jump!

Eight hundred meters between us. At that range my exhaust should have been melting it to ions.

Six hundred meters. *Kali* was whole again.

JUMP!

I jumped. *Zombie* leapt blindly out of space. For one sickening moment, geometry died. Then the vortex spat me out.

But not alone.

We came through together. Cat and mouse dropped into reality four hundred meters apart, coasting at about one-thousandth c. The momentum vectors didn't quite match; within ten seconds *Kali* was over a hundred kilometres away.

Then you destroyed her.

It took some time to figure that out. All I saw was the flash, so bright it nearly overwhelmed the filters; then the cooling shell of hydrogen that crested over me and dissipated into a beautiful, empty sky.

I couldn't believe that I was free.

I tried to imagine what might have caused *Kali*'s destruction. Engine malfunction? Sabotage or mutiny on board, for reasons I could never even guess at? Ritual suicide?

Until I played back the flight recorder, it never occurred to me that she might have been hit by a missile travelling at half the speed of light.

That frightened me more than *Kali* had. The short-range board gave me a clear view to five A.U.s, and there was nothing in any direction. Whatever had destroyed her must have come from a greater distance. It must have been en route before we'd even come through.

It had been expecting us.

I almost missed *Kali* in that moment. At least she hadn't been invisible. At least she hadn't been able to see the future.

There was no way of knowing whether the missile had been

meant for my pursuer, or for me, or for anything else that wandered by. Was I alive because you didn't want me dead, or because you thought I was dead already? And if my presence went undetected now, what might give me away? Engine emissions, RF, perhaps some exotic property of advanced technology which my creators have yet to discover? What did your weapons key on?

I couldn't afford to find out. I shut everything down to bare subsistence, and played dead, and watched.

I've been here for many days now. At last, things are becoming clear.

Mysterious contacts wander space at the limit of *Zombie's* instruments, following cryptic trails. I have coasted through strands of invisible energy that defy analysis. There is also much background radiation here, of the sort *Kali* bled when she died. I have recorded the light of many fusion explosions: some light-hours distant, some less than a hundred thousand kilometres away.

Occasionally, such things happen at close range.

Strange artifacts appear in the paths of missiles sent from some source too distant to see. Almost always they are destroyed; but once, before your missiles reached it, a featureless sphere split into fragments which danced away like dust motes. Only a few of them fell victim to your appetite that time. And once, something that *shimmered*, as wide and formless as an ocean, took a direct hit without disappearing. It limped out of range at less than the speed of light, and you did not send anything to finish the job.

There are things in this universe that even you cannot destroy.

I know what this is. I am caught in a spiderweb. You snatch ships from their travels and deposit them here to face annihilation. I don't know how far you can reach. This is a very small volume of space, perhaps only two or three light-days across. So many ships couldn't blunder across such a tiny reef by accident; you must be bringing them from a much greater distance. I don't know how. Any singularity big enough to manage such a feat would show up on my instruments a hundred light-years away, and I can find nothing. It doesn't matter anyway, now that I know what you are.

You're *Kali*, but much greater. And only now do you make sense to me.

I've stopped trying to reconcile the wisdom of Earthbound experts with the reality I have encountered. The old paradigms are useless. I propose a new one: *technology implies belligerence*.

Tools exist for only one reason: to force the universe into unnatural shapes. They treat nature as an enemy, they are by definition a rebellion against the way things are. In benign environments technology is a stunted, laughable thing, it can't thrive in cultures gripped by belief in natural harmony. What need of fusion reactors if food is already abundant, the climate comfortable? Why force change upon a world which poses no danger?

Back where I come from, some peoples barely developed stone tools. Some achieved agriculture. Others were not content until they had ended nature itself, and still others until they'd built cities in space.

All rested, eventually. Their technology climbed to some complacent asymptote, and stopped — and so they do not stand before you now. Now even my creators grow fat and slow. Their environment mastered, their enemies broken, they can afford more pacifist luxuries. Their machines softened the universe for them, their own contentment robs them of incentive. They forget that hostility and technology climb the cultural ladder together, they forget that it's not enough to be smart.

You also have to be *mean*.

You did not rest. What hellish world did you come from, that drove you to such technological heights? Somewhere near the core, perhaps: stars and black holes jammed cheek to jowl, tidal maelstroms, endless planetary bombardment by comets and asteroids. Some place where no one can pretend that *life* and *war* aren't synonyms. How far you've come.

My creators would call you barbarians, of course. They know nothing. They don't even know me: I'm a recombinant puppet, they say. My solitary contentment is preordained, my choices all imaginary, automatic. Pitiable.

Uncomprehending, even of their own creations. How could they possibly understand you?

But I understand. And understanding, I can act.

I can't escape you. I'd die of old age before I drifted out of this abattoir on my current trajectory. Nor can I jump free, given your ability to snare ships exceeding lightspeed. There's only one course that may keep me alive.

I've traced back along the paths of the missiles you throw; they converge on a point a little less than three light-days ahead. I know where you are.

We're centuries behind you now, but that may change. Even *your* progress won't be endless; and the more of a threat you pose to the rest of us, the more you spur our own advancement. Was that how you achieved your own exalted stature out here? Did you depose some earlier killer god whose attempts to kill you only made you stronger? Do you fear such a fate for yourselves?

Of course you do.

Even my masters may pose a threat, given time; they'll shake off their lethargy the moment they realise that you exist. You can rid yourself of that threat if you exterminate them while they are still weak. To do that, you need to know where they are.

Don't think you can kill me and learn what you need from my ship. I've destroyed any records that survived *Kali's* assault; there weren't many. And I doubt that even you could deduce much from *Zombie's* metallurgical makeup; my creators evolved under a very common type of star. You have no idea where I come from.

But I do.

My ship can tell you some of the technology. Only *I* can tell you where the nest is. And more than that; I can tell you of the myriad systems that Humanity has explored and colonised. I can tell you all about those pampered children of the womb who sent me into the maelstrom on their behalf. You'll learn little of them by examining me, for I was built to differ from the norm.

But you could always *listen* to me. You have nothing to lose.

I will betray them. Not because I bear them any ill will, but because the ethics of loyalty simply don't apply out here. I'm free of the ties that cloud the judgement of lesser creatures; when you're a sterile product of controlled genetics, *kin selection* is a meaningless phrase.

My survival imperative, on the other hand, is as strong as anyone's.

Not automatic after all, you see. *Autonomous*.

I assume that you can understand this transmission. I'm sending it repeatedly in half-second bursts while thrusting. Wait for me; hold your fire.

I'm worth more to you *alive*.

Ready or not, here I come.

Bethlehem

It was her own damn fault.

No. No, that's not right. But Christ, look at this place; what did she expect, living here?

A dried blood stain smears a meter of sidewalk, a rusty backdrop for broken bottles and the twisted skeleton of an old tenspeed. Everything is too big. All this jagged structure, so solid and visible, frightens me. I focus on the stain, search for some hint of its unseen complexity. I want to throw myself down through familiar orders of magnitude and see *inside*; dead erythrocytes, molecules of ferrous haemoglobin, single atoms dancing in comforting envelopes of quantum uncertainty.

But I can't. It's just a featureless brown blot, and all I can see is that it was once part of someone like me.

She's not answering. I've been buzzing for five minutes now.

I'm the only one in sight, sole occupant of a narrow window in time: all the victims have made for cover, and the monsters aren't out yet. But they're coming, Darwin's agents, always ready to weed out the unfit.

I push the buzzer again. "Jan, it's Keith." Why doesn't she answer? Maybe she can't, maybe someone got in, maybe …

Maybe she just wants to be alone. That's what she said on the phone, isn't it?

So why am I here? It's not that I didn't believe her, exactly. It's not even that I'm worried about her safety. It's more a matter of procedure; when your best friend has been raped, you're supposed to be supportive. That's the rule, even these days. And Janet is my friend, by any practical definition of the term.

Glass breaks somewhere in the distance.

"Jan—"

If I leave now I can still make it back before it gets too late.

The sun doesn't go down for at least another twenty minutes. This was a stupid idea anyway.

I turn away from the gate, and something clicks behind me. I look back; a green light glows by the buzzer. I touch the grating, briefly, jerking my hand back after the slightest contact. Again, for longer this time. No shock. The gate swings inward.

Still no words from the speaker.

"Jan?" I say into the street.

After a moment, she answers. "Come on up, Keith. I — I'm glad you came by …"

Five floors high, Janet bolts the door behind me. The wall holds her up while I step past.

Her footsteps trail me down the hall, stiff, shuffling. In the living room she passes without eye contact, heading for the fridge. "Something to drink?"

"There's a choice?"

"Not much of one. No dairy products, the truck got hijacked again. They had beer, though." Her voice is strong, vibrant even, but she walks as though rigor mortis has already taken hold. Every movement seems painful.

The room is dimly lit; a lamp with an orange shade in one corner, a TV with the volume down. When she opens the fridge, bluish light spills across the bruises on her face. One of her eyes is swollen and pulpy.

She closes the refrigerator. Her face falls into merciful eclipse. She straightens in stages, turns to face me, bottle in hand. I take it without a word, careful not to touch her.

"You didn't have to come," she says. "I'm doing okay."

I shrug. "I just thought, if you needed anything …"

Janet smiles through the swelling. Even that seems to hurt. "Thanks, but I picked up some stuff coming back from the precinct."

"Janet, I'm sorry." How else can you say it?

"It wasn't your fault. It was mine."

I should disagree. I want to disagree.

"It was," she insists, although I haven't spoken. "I should

have seen it coming. Simple scenario, predictable outcome. I should have known."

"Christ, Jan, why are you still living out here?" It sounds like an accusation.

She looks through the window. By now it's dark enough to see the fires on the east side.

"I lived here before," she reminds me. "I'm not going to let the fuckers drive me out now."

Before. I follow her gaze, see a tiny dark spot on the sidewalk below. Families lived here once. It's April. Warm enough that kids would be playing out there now. There are people who think that somewhere, they still do. Somewhere at right angles to this twisted place, some place where the probability wave broke onto a more peaceful reality. I wish I could believe that. There would be a little solace in the thought that in some other timeline, children are playing just outside.

But that world, if it even exists, diverged from ours a long time ago. Three, maybe four years …

"It happened so fast," I murmur.

"Fold catastrophe." Absently, Janet speaks to the window. "Change isn't gradual, Keith, you keep forgetting. Things just cruise along until they hit a breakpoint, and zap: new equilibrium. Like falling off a cliff."

This is how she sees the world: not reality, but a trajectory in phase space. Her senses gather the same data as mine, yet everything she sees sounds so alien …

"What cliff?" I ask her. "What breakpoint? What's *breaking*?"

"What, you don't believe what they say?"

They say a lot of things. With perfect hindsight, they moan about the inevitable collapse of an economy based on perpetual growth. Or they blame an obscenely successful computer virus, a few lines of code that spread worldwide and turned the global economy to static overnight. They say it isn't their fault.

"Twenty years ago they'd be blaming alligators in the sewers," I remark.

Janet starts to speak; her voice erupts in a great wracking cough. She wipes her mouth with the back of her hand, winces. "Well, if you'd prefer, there's always Channel 6's interpretation," she says, pointing to the TV.

I look at her, quizzical.

"The Second Coming. We're almost up to crucifixion plus two thousand years."

I shake my head. "Doesn't make any less sense than most of the stuff I've heard."

"Well."

Mutual discomfort rises around us.

"Well, then," I say at last, turning to leave. "I'll come by tomorrow, see how you're doing—"

She gives me a look. "Come on, boss. You know you're not going anywhere tonight. You wouldn't even make it to Granville."

I open my mouth to protest. She pre-empts me: "There's a bus goes by around eight every morning, one of those new retrofits with the fullerene plating. Almost safe, if you don't mind being a couple of hours late for work."

Jan frowns for a second, as though struck by sudden realization.

"I think I'll work at home for a few days, though," she adds. "If that's okay."

"Don't be ridiculous. Take some time off. Relax."

"Actually, I doubt that I'll really be in the mood to relax."

"I mean—"

She manages another smile. "I appreciate the gesture, Keith, but sitting around just wallowing … it would drive me crazy. I want to work. I *have* to work."

"Jan—"

"It's no big deal. I'll log on tomorrow, just for a minute or two. Should be able to download what I need before any bugs get in, and I'll be set for the rest of the day. Okay?"

"Okay." I'm relieved, of course. At least I've got the good grace to be ashamed about it.

"In the meantime" —she takes a wooden step towards the hall closet— "I'll make up the couch for you."

"Listen, don't worry about anything. Just go lie down, I'll make supper."

"None for me. I'm not hungry."

"Well, okay." Damn. I don't know what else I'm supposed to do. "Do you want me to call anyone? Family, or—"

"No. That's fine, Keith." There's just a hint of caution in her voice. "Thanks anyway."

I let it lie. This is why we're so close. Not because we share the same interests, or are bound by a common passion of scientific discovery, or even because I sometimes give her senior authorship on our papers. It's because we don't intrude or pry or try to figure each other out. There's an unspoken recognition of limits, an acceptance. There's complete trust, because we never tell each other anything.

I'm down in the real world when I hear her name.

It happens, occasionally. Sounds filter down from the huge clumsy universe where other people live; I can usually avoid hearing them. Not this time. There are too many of them, and they're all talking about Janet.

I try to keep working. Phospholipids, neatly excised from a single neuron, lumber like crystalline behemoths across my field of vision. But the voices outside won't shut up, they're dragging me up there with them. I try to block them out, cling to the molecules that surround me, but it doesn't work. Ions recede into membranes, membranes into whole cells, physics to chemistry to sheer gross morphology.

The microscope still holds its image, but I'm outside of it now. I shut off the eyephones, blink at a room crowded with machines and the pithed circuitry of a half-dissected salamander.

The lounge is just down the hall from my office. People in there are talking about rape, talking about Jan's misfortune as though it was somehow rare or exotic. They trade tales of personal violation like old war stories, try to outdo each other with incantations of sympathy and outrage.

I don't understand the commotion. Janet is just another victim of the odds; crime waves and quantum waves have that much in common. There are a million unrealized worlds in which she would have escaped unscathed. In a different million, she would have been killed outright. But this is the one we observed. Here, yesterday, she was only brutalized, and today it will probably be someone else.

Why do they keep going on like this? Is talking about it all day going to get any of us into a universe where such things don't happen?

Why can't they just leave it alone?

"No fucking convergence!" she yells from the living room. The power is off again; she storms down the hall towards me, a frenetic silhouette backlit by the reflected light of distant fires. "Singular Hessian, it says! I worked on the chiasma maps for five fucking hours and I couldn't even get the stats to work, and now the fucking power goes out!"

She pushes a printout into my hands. It's a blurry shadow in the dark. "Where's your flashlight?" I ask.

"Batteries are dead. Fucking typical. Hang on a sec." I follow her back into the living room. She kneels at a corner cabinet, roots through its interior; assorted small objects bounce onto the floor to muffled expressions of disgust.

Her damaged arm exceeds some limit, goes rigid. She cries out. I come up behind. "Are—"

Janet puts one hand behind her, palm out, pushing at the space between us. "I'm okay." She doesn't turn around.

I wait for her to move.

After a moment she gets up, slowly. Light flares in her palm. She sets a candle on the coffee table. The light is feeble, but enough to read by.

"I'll show you," she says, reaching for the printout.

But I've already seen it. "You've confounded two of your variables."

She stops. "What?"

"Your interaction term. It's just a linear transform of action potential and calcium."

She takes the paper from my hand, studies it a moment. "Shit. That's it." She scowls at the numbers, as though they might have changed when I looked at them. "What a fucking stupid mistake."

There's a brief, uncomfortable silence. Then Janet crushes the printout into a ball and throws it at the floor.

"Fucking *stupid*!"

She turns away from me and glares out the window.

I stand there like an idiot and wonder what to do.

And suddenly the apartment comes back to life around us. The living room lights, revived by some far-off and delinquent generator, flicker and then hold steady. Jan's TV blares grainy light and faint, murky sound from the corner. I turn towards it, grateful for the distraction.

The screen offers me a woman, about Janet's age but empty somehow, wearing the shell-shocked look you see everywhere these days. I catch a flash of metal around her wrists before the view changes, shows us the twisted, spindly corpse of an infant with too many fingers. A lidless third eye sits over the bridge of its nose, like a milky black marble embedded in plasticine.

"Hmm," Janet says. "Copy errors."

She's watching the television. My stomach unclenches a bit. This month's infanticide stats crawl up the screen like a weather report.

"Polydactyly *and* a pineal eye. You didn't used to see so many random copy errors."

I don't see her point. Birth defects are old news; they've been rising ever since things started falling apart. Every now and then one of the networks makes the same tired connection, blames everything on radiation or chemicals in the water supply, draws ominous parallels with the fall of Rome.

At least it's got her talking again.

"I bet it's happening to other information systems too," she muses, "not just genetic ones. Like all those viruses in the net; you can't log on for two minutes these days without something trying to lay its eggs in your files. Same damn thing, I bet."

I can't suppress a nervous laugh. Janet cocks her head at me.

"Sorry," I say. "It's just — you never give up, you know? You'd go crazy if you went a day without being able to find a pattern somewhere—"

And suddenly I know why she lives here, why she won't hide with the rest of us up on campus. She's a missionary in enemy territory. She's defying chaos, she is proclaiming her faith; even here, she is saying, there are rules and the universe will damn well make sense. It will behave.

Her whole life is a search for order. No fucking way is she

going to let something as, as *random* as rape get in the way. Violence is noise, nothing more; Janet's after signal. Even now, she's after signal.

I suppose that's a good sign.

The signal crashes along the neuron like a tsunami. Ions in its path stand at sudden attention. A conduit forms, like a strip of mountain range shaking itself flat; the signal spills into it. Electricity dances along the optic nerve and lights up the primitive amphibian brain from an endless millimeter away.

Backtrack the lightning to its source. Here, in the tangled circuitry on the retina; the fading echo of a single photon. A lone quantum event, reaching up from the real world and into my machines. Uncertainty made flesh.

I made it happen, here in my lab. Just by watching. If a photon emits in the forest and there's no one to see it, it doesn't exist.

This is how the world works: nothing is real until someone looks at it. Even the subatomic fragments of our own bodies don't exist except as probability waves; it takes an act of conscious observation at the quantum level to collapse those waves into something solid. The whole universe is unreal at its base, an infinite and utterly hypothetical void but for a few specks where someone's passing glance congeals the mix.

It's no use arguing. Einstein tried. Bohm tried. Even Schrödinger, that hater of cats, tried. But our brains didn't evolve to cope with the space between atoms. You can't fight numbers; a century of arcane quantum mathematics doesn't leave any recourse to common sense.

A lot of people still can't accept it. They're afraid of the fact that nothing is real, so they claim that everything is. They say we're surrounded by parallel worlds just as real as this one, places where we won the Guerre de la Separatiste or the Houston Inferno never happened, an endless comforting smorgasbord of alternative realities. It sounds silly, but they really don't have much choice. The parallel universe schtick is the only consistent alternative to nonexistence, and nonexistence terrifies them.

It empowers me.

I can shape reality, just by looking at it. Anyone can. Or I can avert my eyes, respect its privacy, leave it unseen and totipotent. The thought makes me a little giddy. I can almost forget how far I'm slipping behind, how much I need Janet's hand to guide me, because down here in the real world it doesn't have to matter. Nothing is irrevocable until observed.

She buzzes me through on the first ring. The elevator's acting strangely today; it opens halfway, closes, opens again like an eager mouth. I take the stairs.

The door opens while I'm raising my hand to knock. She stands completely still.

"He came back," she says.

No. Even these days, the odds are just too—

"He was right there. He did it again." Her voice is completely expressionless. She locks the door, leads me down the shadowy hallway.

"He got in? How? Where did he—"

Gray light spills into her living room. We're up against the wall, off to one side of her window. I look around the edge of the curtain, down at the deserted street.

She points outside. "He was right there, he did it again, he did it again—"

To someone else. That's what she means.

Oh.

"She was so stupid," Janet's fingers grip the threadbare curtain, clenching, unclenching. "She was out there all alone. Stupid bitch. Should have seen it coming."

"When did it happen?"

"I don't know. A couple of hours."

"Did anyone—" I ask, because of course I can't say *Did you* —

"No. I don't think anybody else even saw it." She releases the curtain. "She got off easy, all things considered. She walked away."

I don't ask whether the phone lines were up. I don't ask if Janet tried to help, if she shouted or threw something or even let the woman inside afterwards. Janet's not stupid.

A distant mirage sparkles in the deepening twilight: the campus. There's another oasis, a bit nearer, over by False Creek, and the edge of a third if I crane my neck. Everything else is grey or black or flickering orange.

Gangrene covers the body. Just a few remnant tissues still alive.

"You're sure it was the same guy?" I wonder.

"*Who the fuck cares!*" she screams. She catches herself, turns away. Her fists ball up at her sides.

Finally, she turns back to look at me.

"Yes it was," she says in a tight voice. "I'm sure."

I never know what I'm supposed to do.

I know what I'm supposed to feel, though. My heart should go out to her, to anyone so randomly brutalized. This much should be automatic, unthinking. Suddenly I can see her face, really see it, a fragile mask of control teetering on the edge of meltdown; and so much more behind, held barely in check. I've never seen her look like this before, even the day it happened to her. Maybe I just didn't notice. I wait for it to affect me, to fill me with love or sympathy or even pity. She needs something from me. She's my friend. At least that's what I call her. I look for something, anything, that would make me less of a liar. I go down as deep as I can, and find nothing but my own passionate curiosity.

"What do you want me to do?" I ask. I can barely hear my own voice

Something changes in her face. "Nothing. Nothing, Keith. This is something I've got to work through on my own, you know?"

I shift my weight and try to figure out whether she means it.

"I could stay here for a few days," I say at last. "If you want."

"Sure." She looks out the window, her face more distant than ever. "Whatever you like."

"They lost Mars!" he wails, grabbing me by the shoulders.

I know the face; he's about three doors down the hall. But I can't remember the name, it's … wait, Chris, Chris something … Fletcher. That's it.

"All the Viking data," he's saying, "from the 70's, you know, NASA said they had it archived, they said I could have it no problem, I planned my whole fucking *thesis* around it!"

"It got lost?" It figures; data files everywhere are corrupting in record numbers these days.

"No, they know exactly where it is. I can go down and pick it up any time I want," Fletcher says bitterly.

"So what's—"

"It's all on these big magnetic disks—"

"*Magnetic?*"

"—and of course magmedia have been obsolete for fucking *decades*, and when NASA upgraded their equipment they somehow missed the Viking data." He pounds the wall, emits a hysterical little giggle. "So they've got all this data that nobody can access. There probably isn't a computer stodgy enough anywhere on the continent."

I tell Janet about it afterwards. I expect her to shake her head and make commiserating noises, *that's too bad* or *what an awful thing to happen*. But she doesn't even look away from the window. She just nods, and says, "Loss of information. Like what happened to me."

I look outside. No stars visible, of course. Just sullen amber reflections on the bottom of the clouds.

"I can't even remember being raped," she remarks. "Funny, you'd think it would be one of those things that stick in your mind. And I know it happened, I can remember the context and the aftermath and I can piece the story together, but I've lost the actual ... event ..."

From behind, I can see the curve of her cheek and the edge of a smile. I haven't seen Janet smile in a long time. It seems like years.

"Can you prove that the earth revolves around the sun?" she asks. "Can you prove it's not the other way around?"

"What?" I circle to her left, a wary orbit. Her face comes into view, smooth and almost unmarked by now, like a mask.

"You can't, can you? If you ever could. It's been erased. Or maybe it's just lost. We've all forgotten so much ..."

She's so calm. I've never seen her so calm. It's almost frightening.

"You know, I'll bet after a while we forget things as fast as we learn them," she remarks. "I bet that's always the way it's been."

"Why do you say that?" I keep my voice carefully neutral.

"You can't store everything, there's not enough room. How can you take in the new without writing over the old?"

"Come on, Jan." I try for a light touch: "Our brains are running out of disk space?"

"Why not? We're finite."

Jesus, she's serious.

"Not *that* finite. We don't even know what most of the brain does, yet."

"Maybe it doesn't do anything. Maybe it's like our DNA, maybe most of it's junk. You remember back when they found—"

"I remember." I don't want to hear what they found, because I've been trying to forget it for years. They found perfectly healthy people with almost no brain tissue. They found people living among us, heads full of spinal fluid, making do with a thin lining of nerve cells where their brains should be. They found people growing up to be engineers and schoolteachers before discovering that they should have been vegetables instead.

They never found any answers. God knows they looked hard enough. I heard they were making some progress, though, before—

Loss of information, Jan says. Limited disk space. She's still smiling at me, insight shines from her eyes with a giddy radiance. But I can see her vision now, and I don't know what she's smiling about. I see two spheres expanding, one within the other, and the inner one is gaining. The more I learn the more I lose, my own core erodes away from inside. All the basics, dissolving; how *do* I know that the earth orbits the sun?

Most of my life is an act of faith.

I'm half a block from safety when he drops down on me from a second-story window. I get lucky; he makes a telltale noise on the way down. I almost get out of his way. We graze each other and he lands hard on the pavement, twisting his ankle.

Technically, handguns are still illegal. I pull mine out and shoot him in the stomach before he can recover.

A flicker of motion. Suddenly on my left, a woman as big as me, face set and sullen, standing where there was only pavement a moment ago. Her hands are buried deep in the pockets of a torn overcoat. One of them seems to be holding something.

Weapon or bluff? Particle or wave? Door number one or door number two?

I point the gun at her. I try very hard to look like someone who hasn't just used his last bullet. For one crazy moment I think that maybe it doesn't even matter what happens here, whether I live or die, because maybe there *is* a parallel universe, some impossible angle away, where everything works out fine.

No. Nothing happens unless observed. Maybe if I just look the other way ...

She's gone, swallowed by the same alley that disgorged her. I step over the gurgling thing twitching on the sidewalk.

"You can't stay here," I tell Janet when I reach her refuge. "I don't care how many volts they pump through the fence, this place isn't safe."

"Sure it is," she says. She's got the TV tuned to Channel 6, God's own mouthpiece coming through strong and clear; the Reborns have a satellite up in geosynch and that fucker *never* seems to go offline.

She's not watching it, though. She just sits on her sofa, knees drawn up under her chin, staring out the window.

"The security's better on campus," I say. "We can make room for you. And you won't have to commute."

Janet doesn't answer. Inside the TV, a talking head delivers a lecture on the Poisoned Fruits Of Secular Science.

"Jan—"

"I'm okay, Keith. Nobody's gotten in yet."

"They will. All they've got to do is throw a rubber mat over the fence and they're past the first line of defense. Sooner or later they'll crack the codes for the front gate, or—"

"No, Keith. That would take too much planning."

"Janet, I'm telling you—"

"Nothing's organized any more, Keith. Haven't you noticed?"

Several faint explosions echo from somewhere outside.

"I've noticed," I tell her.

"For the past four years," she says, as though I haven't spoken, "all the patterns have just ... fallen apart. Things are getting so hard to predict, lately, you know? And even when you see them coming, you can't do anything about them."

She glances at the television, where the head is explaining that evolution contradicts the Second Law of Thermodynamics.

"It's sort of funny, actually," Janet says.

"What is?"

"Everything. Second Law." She gestures at the screen. "Entropy increasing, order to disorder. Heat death of the universe. All that shit."

"Funny?"

"I mean, life's a pretty pathetic affair in the face of physics. It *is* sort of a miracle it ever got started in the first place."

"Hey." I try for a disarming smile. "You're starting to sound like a creationist."

"Yeah, well in a way they're right. Life and entropy just don't get along. Not in the long run, anyway. Evolution's just a — a holding action, you know?"

"I know, Jan."

"It's like this, this torrent screaming through time and space, tearing everything apart. And sometimes these little pockets of information form in the eddies, in these tiny protected backwaters, and sometimes they get complicated enough to wake up and brag about beating the odds. Never lasts, though. Takes too much energy to fight the current."

I shrug. "That's not exactly news, Jan."

She manages a brief, tired smile. "Yeah, I guess not. Undergrad existentialism, huh? It's just that everything's so … hungry now, you know?"

"Hungry?"

"People. Biological life in general. The Net. That's the whole problem with complex systems, you know; the more intricate they get, the harder entropy tries to rip them apart. We need more and more energy just to keep in one piece."

She glances out the window.

"Maybe a bit more," she says, "than we have available these days."

Janet leans forward, aims a remote control at the television.

"You're right, though. It's all old news."

The smile fades. I'm not sure what replaces it.

"It just never sunk in before, you know?"

Exhaustion, maybe.

She presses the remote. The head fades to black, cut off in mid-rant. A white dot flickers defiantly on center stage for a moment.

"There he goes." Her voice hangs somewhere between irony and resignation. "Washed downstream."

The doorknob rotates easily in my grasp, clockwise, counter-clockwise. It's not locked. A television laughs on the far side of a wall somewhere.

I push the door open.

Orange light skews up from the floor at the far end of the hall, where the living room lamp has fallen. Her blood is every-where, congealing on the floor, crowding the wall with sticky rivulets, thin dark pseudopods that clot solid while crawling for the baseboards—

No.

I push the door open.

It swings in a few centimeters, then jams. Something on the other side yields a bit, sags back when I stop pushing. Her hand is visible through the gap in the doorway, palm up on the floor, fin-gers slightly clenched like the limbs of some dead insect. I push at the door again; the fingers jiggle lifelessly against the hardwood.

No. Not that either.

I push the door open.

They're still in there with her. Four of them. One sits on her couch, watching television. One pins her to the floor. One rapes her. One stands smiling in the hallway, waves me in with a hand wrapped in duct tape, a jagged blob studded with nails and broken glass.

Her eyes are open. She doesn't make a sound—

No. No. No.

These are mere possibilities. I haven't actually *seen* any of them. They haven't happened yet. The door is still closed.

I push it open.

The probability wave collapses.

And the winner is …

None of the above. It's not even her apartment. It's our office.

I'm inside the campus perimeter, safe behind carbon-laminate concrete, guarded by armed patrols and semi-intelligent security systems that work well over half the time. I will not call her, even if the phones are working today. I refuse to indulge these sordid little backflips into worlds that don't even exist.

I am not losing it.

Her desk has been abandoned for two weeks now. The adjacent concrete wall, windowless, unpainted, is littered with nostalgic graphs and printouts; population cycles, fractal intrusions into Ricker curves, a handwritten reminder that *All tautologies are tautologies.*

I don't know what's happening. We're changing. *She's* changing. Of course, you idiot, she was raped, how could she *not* change? But it's as though her attacker was only a catalyst, somehow, a trigger for some transformation still ongoing, cryptic and opaque. She's shrouded in a chrysalis; something's happening in there, I see occasional blurred movement, but all the details are hidden.

I need her for so much. I need her ability to impose order on the universe, I need her passionate desire to reduce everything to triviality. No result was good enough, everything was always too proximate for her; every solution she threw back in my face: "yes, but *why?*" It was like collaborating with a two-year-old.

I've always been a parasite. I feel like I've lost the vision in one eye.

I guess it was ironic. Keith Elliot, quantum physiologist, who saw infinite possibilities in the simplest units of matter; Janet Thomas, catastrophe theorist, who reduced whole ecosystems down to a few lines of computer code. We should have killed each other. Somehow it was a combination that worked.

Oh God. When did I start using past tense?

There's a message on the phone, ten hours old. The impossible has happened; the police caught someone, a suspect. His mug shots are on file in the message cache.

He looks a bit like me.

"Is that him?" I ask her.

"I don't know." Janet doesn't look away from the window. "I didn't look."

"Why not? Maybe he's the one! You don't even have to leave the apartment, you could just call them back, say yes or no. Jan, what's going on with you?"

She cocks her head to one side. "I think," she says, "My eyes have opened. Things have finally started to make some sort of … sense, I guess—"

"Christ, Janet, you were *raped*, not baptized!"

She draws her knees up under her chin and starts rocking back and forth. I can't call it back.

I try anyway. "Jan, I'm sorry. It's just … I don't understand, you don't seem to care about *anything* any more—"

"I'm not pressing charges." Rocking, rocking. "Whoever it was. It wasn't his fault."

I can't speak.

She looks back over her shoulder. "Entropy increases, Keith. You know that. Every act of random violence helps the universe run down."

"What are you talking about? Some asshole deliberately assaulted you!"

She shrugs, looking back out the window. "So some matter is sentient. That doesn't exempt it from the laws of physics."

I finally see it; in this insane absolution she confers, in the calm acceptance in her voice. Metamorphosis is complete. My anger evaporates. Underneath there is only a sick feeling I can't name.

"Jan," I say, very quietly.

She turns and faces me, and there is no reassurance there at all.

"*Things fall apart*," she says. "*The center cannot hold. Mere anarchy is loosed upon the world.*"

It sounds familiar, somehow, but I can't … I can't …

"Nothing? You've forgotten Yeats, too?" She shakes her head, sadly. "You taught it to me."

I sit beside her. I touch her, for the first time. I take her hands. She doesn't look at me. But she doesn't seem to mind.

"You'll forget everything, soon, Keith. You'll even forget me."

She looks at me then, and something she sees makes her smile a little. "You know, in a way I envy you. You're still safe from all this. You look so closely at everything you barely see anything at all."

"Janet …"

But she seems to have forgotten me.

After a moment she takes her hands from mine and stands up. Her shadow, cast orange by the table lamp, looms huge and ominous on the far wall. But it's her face, calm and unscarred and only life-sized, that scares me.

She reaches down, puts her hands on my shoulders. "Keith, thank you. I could never have come through this without you. But I'm okay now, and I think it's time to be on my own again."

A pit opens in my stomach. "You're not okay," I tell her, but I can't seem to keep my voice level.

"I'm fine, Keith. Really. I honestly feel better than I have in … well, in a long time. It's all right for you to go."

I can't. I can't.

"I really think you're wrong." I have to keep her talking. I have to stay calm. "You may not see it but I don't think you should be on your own just yet, you can't do this—"

Her eyes twinkle briefly. "Can't do what, Keith?"

I try to answer but it's hard, I don't even know what I'm trying to say, I—

"*I* can't do it," is what comes out, unexpected. "It's just us, Janet, against everything. I can't do it without you."

"Then don't try."

It's such a stupid thing to say, so completely unexpected, that I have no answer for it.

She draws me to my feet. "It's just not that important, Keith. We study retinal sensitivity in salamanders. Nobody cares. Why should they? Why should *we*?"

"You know it's more than that, Janet! It's quantum neurology, it's the whole nature of consciousness, it's—"

"It's really kind of pathetic, you know." Her smile is so gentle, her voice so kind, that it takes a moment for me to actually realize what she's saying. "You can change a photon here and there, so you tell yourself you've got some sort of control over things. But you don't. None of us do. It all just got too complicated, it's all just physics—"

My hand is stinging. There's a sudden white spot, the size of my palm, on the side of Janet's face. It flushes red as I watch.

She touches her cheek. "It's okay, Keith. I know how you feel. I know how everything feels. We're so tired of swimming upstream all the time …"

I see her, walking on air.

"You need to get out of here," I say, talking over the image. "You should really spend some time on campus, I could put you up until you get your bearings—"

"Shhhhh." She puts a finger to my lips, guides me along the hall. "I'll be fine, Keith. And so will you. Believe me. This is all for the best."

She reaches past me and opens the door.

"I love you," I blurt out.

She smiles at that, as though she understands. "Goodbye, Keith."

She leaves me there and turns back down the hall. I can see part of her living room from where I stand, I can see her turn and face the window. The firelight beyond paints her face like a martyr's. She never stops smiling. Five minutes go by. Ten. Perhaps she doesn't realize I'm still here, perhaps she's forgotten me already.

At last, when I finally turn to leave, she speaks. I look back, but her eyes are still focused on distant wreckage, and her words are not meant for me.

"… *what rough beast* …" is what I think she says, and other words too faint to make out.

When the news hits the department I try, unsuccessfully, to stay out of sight. They don't know any next of kin, so they inflict their feigned sympathy on me. It seems she was popular. I never knew that. Colleagues and competitors pat me on the back as though Janet and I were lovers. Sometimes it happens, they say, as though imparting some new insight. Not your fault. I endure their commiseration as long as I can, then tell them I want to be alone. This, at least, they think they understand; and now, my knuckles stinging from a sudden collision of flesh and glass, now I'm free. I dive into the eyes of my microscope, escaping down, down into the real world.

I used to be so much better than everyone. I spent so much time down here, nose pressed against the quantum interface, embracing uncertainties that would drive most people insane. But I'm not at ease down here. I never was. I'm simply more terrified of the world outside.

Things happen out there, and can't be taken back. Janet is gone, forever. I'll never see her again. That wouldn't happen down here. Down here nothing is impossible. Janet is alive as well as dead; I made a difference, and didn't; parents make babies and monsters and both and neither. Everything that can be, is. Down here, riding the probability wave, my options stay open forever.

As long as I keep my eyes closed.

Home

It has forgotten what it was.

Not that that matters, down here. What good is a name when there's nothing around to use it? This one doesn't remember where it came from. It doesn't remember the murky twilight of the North Pacific Drift, or the noise and gasoline aftertaste that drove it back below the thermocline. It doesn't remember the gelatinous veneer of language and culture that once sat atop its spinal cord. It doesn't even remember the long slow dissolution of that overlord into dozens of autonomous, squabbling subroutines. Now, even those have fallen silent.

Not much comes down from the cortex any more. Low-level impulses flicker in from the parietal and occipital lobes. The motor strip hums in the background. Occasionally, Broca's area mutters to itself. The rest is mostly dead and dark, worn smooth by a sluggish black ocean cold as antifreeze. All that's left is pure reptile.

It pushes on, blind and unthinking, oblivious to the weight of four hundred liquid atmospheres. It eats whatever it can find. Desalinators and recyclers keep it hydrated. Sometimes, old mammalian skin grows sticky with secreted residues; newer skin, laid on top, opens pores to the ocean and washes everything clean with aliquots of distilled sea water.

The reptile never wonders about the signal in its head that keeps it pointing the right way. It doesn't know where it's headed, or why. It only knows, with pure brute instinct, how to get there.

It's dying, of course, but slowly. It wouldn't care much about that even if it knew.

Now something is tapping on its insides. Infinitesimal, precisely spaced shock waves are marching in from somewhere ahead and drumming against the machinery in its chest.

The reptile doesn't recognize the sound. It's not the intermittent grumble of conshelf and sea bed pushing against each other. It's not the low-frequency ATOC pulses that echo dimly past en route to the Bering. It's a pinging noise — *metallic*, Broca's area murmurs, although it doesn't know what that means.

Abruptly, the sound intensifies.

The reptile is blinded by sudden starbursts. It blinks, a vestigial act from a time it doesn't remember. The caps on its eyes darken automatically. The pupils beneath, hamstrung by the speed of reflex, squeeze to pinpoints a few seconds later.

A copper beacon glares out from the darkness ahead — too coarse, too steady, far brighter than the bioluminescent embers that sometimes light the way. Those, at least, are dim enough to see by; the reptile's augmented eyes can boost even the faint twinkle of deepwater fish and turn it into something resembling twilight. But this new light turns the rest of the world stark black. Light is never this bright, not since—

From the cortex, a shiver of recognition.

It floats motionless, hesitating. It's almost aware of faint urgent voices from somewhere nearby. But it's been following the same course for as long it can remember, and that course points only one way.

It sinks to the bottom, stirring a muddy cloud as it touches down. It crawls forward along the ocean floor.

The beacon shines down from several meters above the sea bed. At closer range it resolves into a string of smaller lights stretched in an arc, like photophores on the flank of some enormous fish.

Broca sends down more noise: *Sodium floods*. The reptile burrows on through the water, panning its face from side to side.

And freezes, suddenly fearful. Something huge looms behind the lights, bloating gray against black. It hangs above the sea bed like a great smooth boulder, impossibly buoyant, encircled by lights at its equator. Striated filaments connect it to the bottom.

Something else, changes.

It takes a moment for the reptile to realize what's happened: the drumming against its chest has stopped. It glances nervously from shadow to light, light to shadow.

"You are approaching Linke Station, Aleutian Geothermal Array. We're glad you've come back."

The reptile shoots back into the darkness, mud billowing behind it. It retreats a good twenty meters before a dim realization sinks in.

Broca's area knows those sounds. It doesn't understand them — Broca's never much good at anything but mimicry — but it has heard something like them before. The reptile feels an unaccustomed twitch. It's been a long time since curiosity was any use.

It turns and faces back from where it fled. Distance has smeared the lights into a diffuse, dull glow. A faint staccato rhythm vibrates in its chest.

The reptile edges back towards the beacon. One light divides again into many; that dim, ominous outline still lurks behind them.

Once more the rhythm falls silent at the reptile's approach. The strange object looms overhead in its girdle of light. It's smooth in some places, pockmarked in others. Precise rows of circular bumps, sharp-angled protuberances appear at closer range.

"You are approaching Linke Station, Aleutian Geothermal Array. We're glad you've come back."

The reptile flinches, but stays on course this time.

"We can't get a definite ID from your sonar profile." The sound fills the ocean. "You might be Deborah Linden. Deborah Linden. Please respond if you are Deborah Linden."

Deborah Linden. That brings memory: something with four familiar limbs, but standing upright, moving against gravity and bright light and making strange harsh sounds—

—*laughter*—

"Please respond—"

It shakes its head, not knowing why.

"—if you are Deborah Linden."

Judy Caraco, says something else, very close.

"Deborah Linden. If you can't speak, please wave your arms."

The lights overhead cast a bright scalloped circle on the ocean floor. There on the mud rests a box, large enough to crawl into. Two green pinpoints sparkle from a panel on one of its sides.

"Please enter the emergency shelter beneath the station. It contains food and medical facilities."

One end of the box gapes open; delicate jointed things can be seen folded up inside, hiding in shadow.

"Everything is automatic. Enter the shelter and you'll be all right. A rescue team is on the way."

Automatic. That noise, too, sticks out from the others. *Automatic* almost means something. It has personal relevance.

The reptile looks back up at the thing that's hanging overhead like, like,

—*like a fist*—

like a fist. The underside of the sphere is a cool shadowy refuge; the equatorial lights can't reach all the way around its convex surface. In the overlapping shadows on the south pole, something shimmers enticingly.

The reptile pushes up off the bottom, raising another cloud.

"Deborah Linden. The station is locked for your own protection."

It glides into the cone of shadow beneath the object and sees a bright shiny disk a meter across, facing down, held inside a circular rim. The reptile looks up into it.

Something looks back.

Startled, the reptile twists down and away. The disk writhes in the sudden turbulence.

A bubble. That's all it is. A pocket of gas, trapped underneath the —*airlock*.

The reptile stops. It knows that word. It even understands it, somehow. Broca's not alone any more, something else is reaching out from the temporal lobe and tapping in. Something up there actually knows what Broca is talking about.

"Please enter the emergency shelter beneath the station—"

Still nervous, the reptile returns to the airlock. The air

pocket shines silver in the reflected light. A black wraith moves into view within it, almost featureless except for two empty white spaces where eyes should be. It reaches out to meet the reptile's outstretched hand. Two sets of fingertips touch, fuse, disappear. One arm is grafted onto its own reflection at the wrist. Fingers, on the other side of the looking glass, touch metal.

"—locked for your own protection. Deborah Linden."

It pulls back its hand, fascinated. Inside, forgotten parts are stirring. Other parts, more familiar, try to send them away. The wraith floats overhead, empty and untroubled.

It draws its hand to its face, runs an index finger from one ear to the tip of the jaw. A very long molecule, folded against itself, unzips.

The wraith's smooth black face splits open a few centimeters; what's underneath shows pale gray in the filtered light. The reptile feels the familiar dimpling of its cheek in sudden cold.

It continues the motion, slashing its face from ear to ear. A great smiling gash opens below the eyespots. Unzipped, a flap of black membrane floats under its chin, anchored at the throat.

There's a pucker in the center of the skinned area. The reptile moves its jaw; the pucker opens.

By now most of its teeth are gone. It swallowed some, spat others out if they came loose when its face was unsealed. No matter. Most of the things it eats these days are even softer than it is. When the occasional mollusc or echinoderm proves too tough or too large to swallow whole, there are always hands. Thumbs still oppose.

But this is the first time it's actually seen that gaping, toothless ruin where a mouth used to be. It knows this isn't right, somehow.

"—Everything is automatic—"

A sudden muffled buzz cuts into the noise, then fades. Welcome silence returns for a moment. Then different sounds, quieter than before, almost hushed:

"Christ, Judy, is that you?"

It knows that sound.

"Judy Caraco? It's Jeannette Ballard. Remember? We went through prelim together. Judy? Can you speak?"

That sound comes from a long time ago.

"Can you hear me, Judy? Wave if you can hear me."

Back when this one was part of something larger, not an *it* at all, then, but—

"The machine didn't recognize you, you know? It was only programmed for locals."

—*she*.

Clusters of neurons, long dormant, sparkle in the darkness. Old, forgotten subsystems stutter and reboot.

I—

"You've come — my God, Judy, do you know where you are? You went missing off Juan de Fuca! You've come over three thousand kilometers!"

It knows my name. She can barely think over the sudden murmuring in her head.

"Judy, it's me. Jeannette. God, Judy, how did you last this long?"

She can't answer. She's just barely starting to understand the question. There are parts of her still asleep, parts that won't talk, still other parts completely washed away. She doesn't remember why she never gets thirsty. She's forgotten the tidal rush of human breath. Once, for a little while, she knew words like *photoamplification* and *myoelectric*; they were nonsense to her even then.

She shakes her head, trying to clear it. The new parts — no, the old parts, the very old parts that went away and now they've come back *and won't shut the fuck up* — are all clamoring for attention. She reaches into the bubble again, past her own reflection; once again, the ventral airlock pushes back.

"Judy, you can't get into the station. No one's there. Everything's automated now."

She brings her hand back to her face, tugs at the line between black and gray. More shadow peels back from the wraith, leaving a large pale oval with two smaller ovals, white and utterly featureless, inside. The flesh around her mouth is going prickly and numb.

My face! something screams. *What happened to my eyes?*

"You don't want to go inside anyway, you couldn't even stand up. We've seen it in some of the other runaways, you lose your calcium after a while. Your bones go all punky, you know?"

My eyes—

"We're airlifting a 'scaphe out to you. We'll have a team down there in fifteen hours, tops. Just go down into the shelter and wait for them. It's state of the art, Judy, it'll take care of everything."

She looks down into the open box. Words appear in her head: *Leg. Hold. Trap.* She knows what they mean.

"They — they made some mistakes, Judy. But things are different now. We don't have to change people any more. You just wait there, Judy. We'll put you back to rights. We'll bring you home."

The voices inside grow quiet, suddenly attentive. They don't like the sound of that word. *Home.* She wonders what it means. She wonders why it makes her feel so cold.

More words scroll through her mind: *The lights are on. Nobody's home.*

The lights come on, flickering.

She can catch glimpses of sick, rotten things squirming in her head. Old memories grind screeching against years of corrosion. Something lurches into sudden focus: worms, clusters of twitching, eyeless, pulpy snouts reaching out for her across the space of two decades. She stares, horrified, and remembers what the worms were called. They were called "fingers".

Something gives way with a snap. There's a big room and a hand puppet clenched in one small fist. Something smells like mints and worms are surging up between her legs and they *hurt* and they're whispering *shhh it's not really that bad is it*, and it is but she doesn't want to let him down *after all I've done for you* so she shakes her head and squeezes her eyes shut and just waits. It's years and years before she opens her eyes again and when she does he's back, so much smaller now, he doesn't remember he doesn't even fucking *remember* it's all *my dear how you've grown how long has it been?* So she tells him as the taser wires hit and he goes over, she tells him as his muscles lock tight in a twelve thousand volt orgasm; she shows him the blade, shows him up real close and his left eye deflates with a wet tired sigh but she leaves the other one, jiggling hilariously in frantic little arcs, so he can watch but shit for once there really is a cop around when you need one and here come the worms again, a hard clenched knot of them driving into her kidney like a piston, worms grabbing her hair, and they take her not to the nearest precinct but to some strange clinic where voices in the next room murmur about *optimal post-traumatic environments* and *endogenous dopamine addiction.* And then someone says *There's an alternative Ms. Caraco, a place you could go that's a little bit dangerous but then you'd be right at home there, wouldn't you? And you could make a real contribution, we need people who can live under a certain kind of stress without going, you know ...*

And she says *okay, okay, just fucking do it.*

And the worms burrow into her chest, devour her soft parts and replace them with hard-edged geometries of plastic and metal that cut her insides.

And then dark cold, life without breath, four thousand meters of black water pressing down like a massive sheltering womb ...

"Judy, will you just for God's sake *talk* to me? Is your vocoder broken? Can't you answer?"

Her whole body is shaking. She can't do anything except watch her hand rise, an autonomous savior, to take the black skin floating around her face. The reptile presses edges together, here, and here. Hydrophobic side chains embrace; a slippery black caul stitches itself back together over rotten flesh. Muffled voices rage faintly inside.

"Judy, please just *wave* or something! Judy, what are you — where are you going?"

It doesn't know. All it's ever done is travel to this place. It's forgotten why.

"Judy, you can't wander too far away ... don't you remember, our instruments can't see very well this close to an active rift—"

All it wants is to get away from the noise and the light. All it wants is to be alone again.

"Judy, wait — we just want to help—"

The harsh artificial glare fades behind it. Ahead there is only the sparse twinkle of living flashlights.

A faint realization teeters on the edge of awareness and washes away forever:

She knew this was home years before she ever saw an ocean.

Publication History:

"Bulk Food" 2000. *On Spec* 12(2), pgs 173-191.

"Home" 1999. *On Spec* 11(1), pgs 69-75.

"The Second Coming of Jasmine Fitzgerald" 1998. *Divine Realms*, S. MacGregor, Editor. pgs 243-269. Turnstone Books, Regina.

"Bethlehem" 1997. *Tesseracts⁵*, Yves Meynard and Robert Runté, Editors, pgs 274-291. Tesseracts Books, Edmonton.

"Fractals: or, Reagan Assured Gorbachev of Help Against Space Aliens" 1995. On Spec 7(1), pgs 31-41.

"Flesh made word" 1994. *Prairie Fire*, 15(2), pgs 144-157.

"Nimbus" 1993. On Spec 6(2), pgs 8-17.

"A Niche" 1990. *Tesseracts³*, C. J. Dorsey and G. Truscott, Editors, pgs 127-165. Press Porcépic, Victoria. Reprinted in *Northern Stars* (Grant, G. and Hartwell, D.G. eds.), Tor Books, New York. Also in *Aurora Awards* (E. van Belkom, ed.), Quarry Books, Kingston.

"Ambassador" was written especially for this volume!

The harsh artificial glare fades behind it. Ahead there is only the sparse twinkle of living flashlights.

A faint realization teeters on the edge of awareness and washes away forever:

She knew this was home years before she ever saw an ocean.

Publication History:

"Bulk Food" 2000. *On Spec* 12(2), pgs 173-191.

"Home" 1999. *On Spec* 11(1), pgs 69-75.

"The Second Coming of Jasmine Fitzgerald" 1998. *Divine Realms*, S. MacGregor, Editor. pgs 243-269. Turnstone Books, Regina.

"Bethlehem" 1997. *Tesseracts⁵*, Yves Meynard and Robert Runté, Editors, pgs 274-291. Tesseracts Books, Edmonton.

"Fractals: or, Reagan Assured Gorbachev of Help Against Space Aliens" 1995. On Spec 7(1), pgs 31-41.

"Flesh made word" 1994. *Prairie Fire*, 15(2), pgs 144-157.

"Nimbus" 1993. On Spec 6(2), pgs 8-17.

"A Niche" 1990. *Tesseracts³*, C. J. Dorsey and G. Truscott, Editors, pgs 127-165. Press Porcépic, Victoria. Reprinted in *Northern Stars* (Grant, G. and Hartwell, D.G. eds.), Tor Books, New York. Also in *Aurora Awards* (E. van Belkom, ed.), Quarry Books, Kingston.

"Ambassador" was written especially for this volume!

Peter Watts devolved into full-time writing after fifteen years of marine mammal research, undergraduate teaching, and inadvertent academic prostitution. He has won a handful of awards in fields as diverse as biology, documentary, and science fiction; none have made him rich, and at least one (the unfortunately-named "Hoar Award", for excellence in oral presentation) has been an actual embarrassment. His first novel, *Starfish*, was a New York Times Notable Book of the Year. His second novel will be released in 2001. He is presently trapped in Toronto, but hopes to escape to Vancouver before the Fraser Valley is completely paved over.

If you enjoyed this book... sample one of these other fine speculative fiction offerings from Tesseract Books:

Resisting Adonis
by Timothy J. Anderson
ISBN: 1-895836-83-2 (hardcover, $23.95),
          1-895-836-84-0 (paperback, $11.95)

An erotic science fiction thriller debut from the author of the controversial *Neurotic Erotica* (Slipstream, 1996). In a future United North America scarred by genetic warfare, a physically perfect child ignites a black comedy of errors. A renegade orthodontist, a factory worker-turned-supermodel from China, a bag lady and a host of other star-crossed denizens find themselves caught up in an international yet intensely personal story. Tesseract Books, 2000. 256 pp.

The Plague Saint
by Rita Donovan
ISBN: 1-895-836-29-8 (hardcover, $21.95),
          1-895836-28-X (paperback, $9.95)

In the harsh near-future, dominated by religious ideologues and physical plague, Lily Dalriada defies authority when she is arbitrarily chosen to be The Plague Saint, and begins a journey both real and virtual across Canada and through medieval and Renaissance Florence. Rita Donovan is the award-winning author of *Dark Jewels* (1991) and *Daisy Circus* (1993). Tesseract Books, 1997. 156 pp.

Blue Apes
By Phyllis Gotlieb
ISBN: 1-895836-14-X (hardcover, $21.95),
     1-895836-13-1 (paperback, $8.95)
Eleven classic stories from one of Canadian SF's most successful and prolific authors, popular around the world, written over a twenty-year span and collected in one attractive volume. Provocative themes and entertaining characters, both human and alien, abound in this anthology a must for any science fiction reader! Tesseract Books, 1995. 272 pp.

...and don't forget the Tesseracts anthologies! Nine volumes, and counting, of the best in Canadian speculative short fiction since the first Tesseract appeared in 1985, edited by Judith Merril. Experience the thrill of short fiction by both internationally lauded authors such as Atwood, Gibson and Dorsey, and gems by the whole spectrum of Canadian speculative fiction writers, including the landmark *TesseractsQ* anthology of the best in Quebec sf in English translation! Many volumes are available in collector hardcover editions.

Order these and other fine Tesseract Books by writing, faxing or e-mailing Tesseract Books, an imprint of The Books Collective, 214-21, 10405 Jasper Avenue, Edmonton, Alberta, Canada T5J 3S2, telephone (780) 448-0590, fax (780) 448-0640, e-mail <admin@bookscollective.com> or <tesseract@bookscollective.com>.

US customers pay in US dollars. Cheques payable to the Books Collective. MasterCard accepted. Canadian bookstores can order through Literary Press Group / General Distributing (refer to "Coteau catalogue" in your enquiry.) All international enquiries directly to Tesseract Books. Usual bookstore and library discount apply. Add $3 for first book, $1.50 each additional book for shipping and handling. Catalogues available on written request with 8 1 /2 ×11 or A4 SASE.